The Dog with No Name

Pet Finders Club

The Dog with No Name

by Ben M. Baglio

Cover art by Andrew Beckett
Interior art by Meg Aubrey

SCHOLASTIC INC.

New York   Toronto   London   Auckland   Sydney
Mexico City   New Delhi   Hong Kong   Buenos Aires

ISBN 0-439-74617-5

Text copyright © 2004 by Working Partners Limited.
Illustrations copyright © 2004 by Scholastic Inc.

All rights reserved. Published by Scholastic Inc.

12 11 10 9 8 7 6 5 4 3 2   5 6 7 8 9 10/0

Printed in the U.S.A.   40
First Scholastic printing, May 2005

Special thanks to Liss Norton

Thanks also to Jo Raine, VN, Grove Lodge
Veterinary Hospital, for reviewing the veterinary
information contained in this book

The Dog with No Name

Chapter One

"Why exactly did we come this way, Tris?" Andi Talbot demanded as a heavy truck rumbled past on the highway. "Buddy's getting freaked out by all this traffic." The little Jack Russell terrier trotting beside her leaped to the end of his leash, barking madly. She reached down to smooth the fur between his ears.

"Because the best parking lot in the whole city for skateboarding is up here," Tristan replied. "It's wide and smooth, with no manhole covers. Perfect for practicing jumps."

"It's a shame it won't have the best skateboarder in Orchard Park on it," added Natalie Lewis, their best friend.

Making a face at her, Tristan pushed off and sent his skateboard rolling along the sidewalk in front of them. He picked up speed, then leaped off his board and

1

twisted his whole body around. Landing perfectly on the board again, he punched his fists up into the air triumphantly. "Pro-skateboarding, here I come!"

"Wow!" Andi said, impressed.

"My best yet," he agreed, picking up his board and walking back. He bent down to pet Buddy. The terrier had stopped barking, but he still watched the racing traffic closely, flinching when big trucks passed by.

"I bet it was a fluke," said Natalie. "Bet you can't do it again." She flipped her blond hair out of her eyes and laughed. "I can see a spectacular skateboard crash coming any minute now."

Tristan frowned. "I'll do even better this time."

"You'll fall off," Natalie warned.

Tristan stepped onto the board and began to race away.

Andi and Natalie exchanged doubtful glances. "He'll end up breaking his arm or something," Natalie said as he sprang into the air again. She bent down and covered her black Labrador's eyes with her hand. "Don't look, Jet," she joked.

Tristan spun around again, but this time he missed the skateboard completely on the way down. His ankle crumpled underneath him and he staggered backward, flapping his arms as he tried to keep his balance. He stumbled on the steep slope that bordered the sidewalk and went rolling down the grass and out of sight.

Andi and Natalie rushed over with the dogs scampering beside them.

"Are you all right?" Andi called.

There was no reply.

"Tristan!" She reached the place where Tristan had disappeared, then stopped and stared. He was crawling out of a water-filled ditch at the bottom of the slope, his hair and clothes covered with sticky gray mud.

Natalie stood beside Andi, openmouthed.

"I'm all right!" he called up to them, wiping away streaks of grime from his face. "Not hurt at all — in case you were worried."

"Doing your swamp-creature impersonation?" Natalie said.

"Something like that."

"Come on, let's give him a hand," Andi said, trying not to laugh. Wet muck was dripping from Tristan's hair, and there was a piece of a feathery weed stuck to his shoulder.

She began to scramble down the bank toward him.

"I'll only help if he promises not to touch my jacket," Natalie said, stepping carefully after her. Jet and Buddy bounced along on their leashes, as if the ditch were a much more interesting place to be than the sidewalk.

By the time Andi reached Tristan, he was kneeling beside the ditch, wiping his hands on the grass. "Yuck! Look at this stuff!"

"It's called mud, Tristan," Natalie puffed, sliding down the last few feet to join them. "And it's not toxic."

"Do you need a hand getting up?" Andi offered.

"Not until I've emptied my sneakers. There's something wriggling around in one of them. I think I caught a tadpole."

"Gross!" Natalie moaned. Then her face turned very serious. "Then be really careful when you take your shoes off, Tris."

Andi and Tristan stared at her.

"Why?" Tristan asked nervously, stopping in the middle of untying his lace.

"It might not be a tadpole. It might be a fish." Natalie grinned. "I just thought you might want to save it for your mid-morning snack. I mean, it must be an hour and a half since you ate."

"Very funny!" Tristan made a face at Natalie. "I don't eat *that* much."

"That's not really true, is it, Tris?" Andi pointed out. Tristan was famous for being hungry. He knew just about every snack bar and convenience store in Orchard Park.

She was about to remind him of a time when he'd eaten an entire family-size bag of pretzels at once, when Buddy began to whine and pull on his leash.

"What's up, Bud?" Andi asked, looking down at the tan-and-white terrier. "Can't stand seeing Tristan like this?"

Buddy's whine became more urgent. He looked up at Andi and barked sharply.

"What is it, boy?"

"He probably picked up the scent of a pizza box again," Natalie said. "Let's get back to the sidewalk before we end up looking like Tris."

"No, wait. This feels like something different." Andi let Buddy drag her along the bank toward a clump of rough, thorny shrubs.

"What did he find?" Tristan wondered as Buddy rushed up to the bushes, sniffing eagerly.

"I don't know. It could be a duck or something." Andi pulled the sleeves of her jacket down to protect her hands, then pushed her way into the shrubs. Through the dense branches and brambles, she could see something lying at the edge of the ditch, but it was entirely covered in mud so that she couldn't make out what it was. An old sweater? Someone's tote bag?

Buddy looked up at her and whined. Would he really

be this interested in a piece of trash? Andi bent down and pushed some branches aside to see more clearly, then jumped back, shocked. It was a puppy, lying horrifyingly still. "Oh, no!" she gasped.

"What is it?" Natalie called, making her way over. Tristan came limping after her, holding one sneaker in his hand.

"There's a puppy in there," Andi gulped. She parted the branches again, and they all peered through. The puppy was lying half in and half out of the ditch. You couldn't even tell what color it was, underneath all the mud.

"Do you think it's . . . dead?" Natalie whispered.

Before anyone could reply, Buddy quickly made his way through the bushes and touched the puppy's face with his nose. The puppy whimpered weakly and opened one eye.

"It's alive!" Tristan exclaimed. "Come on, we've got to get it out." He threw down his sneaker and shoved his way into the bushes, holding his hands above his head to save himself from being pricked by the thorns.

Natalie pulled out her cell phone. "I'll call Fisher." Fisher Pearce was the vet at the local ASPCA center, and they knew him well. They often bumped into him around town. He was a good friend of Christine Wilson,

Tristan's mom's cousin, who also owned a local pet store.

"Can you hold Buddy, too, Nat?" Andi asked. "I want to help Tris." When Natalie nodded, her cell phone clamped to one ear, Andi handed her Buddy's leash and quickly began trampling through the bushes.

The puppy's ears twitched as they kneeled beside it. "I think she's a Labrador," Andi said. "She's got those thick, floppy ears that Labradors have. And she looks pretty muscular under all that mud." Andi rested her hand on the puppy's broad, rounded forehead; she felt very cold. A tiny pink tongue flicked out under the puppy's nose, as if she wanted to lick Andi's hand.

"It's all right, little one," Andi whispered. "We're going to get you out of here."

Tristan wriggled farther into the bushes, then slid down into the ditch and around the puppy so that he was behind her. "I'll lift her from here. That way — " He broke off. "Hang on! Her back leg's twisted. I don't think we should move her."

"We can't leave her like this!" Andi protested. "She's so cold. Can't we at least lift her out of the thorns?"

"No. It could cause more damage. Let's wait for Fisher."

Andi took off her jacket and laid it over the puppy.

"Don't worry, girl," she said. "You'll be safe soon." She cleared mud away from the tiny Labrador's nose so she could breathe easier, then gently slid her hand under her rib cage, feeling for her heartbeat. She could just make out a faint flutter, but it was nothing like the strong, steady pulse she felt when Buddy lay across her lap.

"I hope Fisher gets here fast," she said. She could hear Natalie talking into the phone, but she couldn't make out what she was saying above the roar of the traffic on the highway above them.

"Do you think she was hit by a car?" Andi wondered, stroking the tiny creature's head.

"Probably," Tristan agreed. "Poor little thing. From the look of all that mud, she must have fallen right into the ditch. She's lucky she managed to pull herself out or she might have drowned, with all this rain we've had."

"I wonder why she was out alone on this busy highway," Andi said.

Tristan shrugged. "Who knows?" He was shivering violently.

"Get out of the ditch, Tris," Andi said. "You look frozen. I know it's spring, but it's not that warm today."

Tristan clambered out, his single sneaker squelching and dingy water dripping from his jeans. "I feel so useless," he muttered, staring down at the motionless puppy.

"Me, too." Andi felt a stab of fear. What if the puppy had died while they'd been talking? She reached under the dog's cold body again, but to her relief the little heart was still beating, though it felt even weaker and more irregular than before. "Hold on, girl!" she whispered.

"We'll have to track down her owners," she stated, trying to stay positive. She, Natalie, and Tristan had organized the Pet Finders Club soon after Andi had moved to Orchard Park, Washington, from Florida last September. Andi had lost Buddy at the same time that Natalie had lost Jet, and the experience had made them realize how terrible it was to lose a pet. So, they'd set up the club to help other people find their missing animals.

Natalie appeared at the end of the path Andi had cleared through the shrubs. "Fisher's on his way."

"Thank goodness," Tristan said. "She looks bad." He rubbed his bare arms, smearing mud over them.

"Here." Natalie slipped off her jacket and handed it to him. "Put this on. You look frozen."

Tristan stared at her in astonishment. "What about all this mud? I'm filthy."

Natalie's clothes always came from the most exclusive boutiques, and she always took great care of them, but she just shrugged. "That doesn't seem important now. I can always take it to the dry cleaner."

Gratefully, Tristan slipped on the jacket. "Thanks, Nat."

"I'll wait at the top of the bank," Natalie said, "so Fisher can find us." She scrambled up the steep slope with Buddy and Jet loping beside her.

Andi went on stroking the puppy, tracing the outline of her tiny floppy ears. Did she even know Andi was there?

About ten minutes passed before Natalie began to wave. "He's here!" she shrieked. "I can see the ASPCA ambulance!"

Andi's heart flipped over with relief. "You'll be okay now, girl," she told the puppy, crossing her fingers for luck.

Fisher appeared at the top of the bank with a backpack slung over his shoulder. He was a tall, dark, friendly-faced man in his early thirties. Behind him came a small, very slim woman with long brown hair tied in a ponytail. She was wearing a white tunic and matching trousers and carrying an armful of blankets. Andi hadn't seen her before, but from her outfit it looked like she worked at the clinic with Fisher.

"How is she?" Fisher called, jogging down the slope. He pushed the bushes aside quickly.

"Not good," Andi said. She moved aside so Fisher could take her place by the puppy's head. He kneeled down and ran his hands gently over the puppy's mud-caked body.

She gave a tiny moan.

"Hang in there, girl," he murmured. "She's badly bruised," he said over his shoulder to Andi. "She might even have some broken bones and internal injuries, too. We'll have to X-ray her to be sure." He sighed. "Poor thing. She's so young — only about ten weeks old, I'd say."

"One of her back legs looks weird," Tristan told him. "Sort of twisted."

Fisher shifted alongside the puppy and ran his hands carefully over the injured leg. The puppy didn't stir.

The woman who'd come with him slid down the bank. She set the blankets on the grass, then made her way into the shrubbery. "Hi, I'm Molly," she said to Andi and Tristan. "I just started at the clinic as a veterinary nurse. I've heard all about you guys." Andi tried to smile, but she was feeling too worried about the pup. Natalie had followed Molly and stood a little way off, keeping Buddy and Jet out of the way. She looked as pale and anxious as Andi felt.

"This hip's dislocated, Molly," Fisher said. "I'll give her a painkilling injection so we can move her."

"Can you fix it?" Andi asked.

"Sure. Dislocated hips look pretty scary, but they don't take long to heal. Though that doesn't necessarily mean she'll be okay, I'm afraid. There could be all sorts of other problems that we don't know about yet."

Andi felt tears well up in her eyes and swallowed hard. *Don't give up yet, girl*, she begged silently. *You're a fighter, I know it!*

Fisher went on. "We'll take her back to the clinic and find out exactly what we're dealing with."

Molly opened a medical kit and took out a hypodermic syringe and a bottle of pale yellow liquid. She filled the syringe, then used a cotton ball moistened with antiseptic to wipe the mud from a small patch on the puppy's neck. "Here you go," she said, handing the syringe to Fisher.

For a moment after he injected the puppy, nothing happened, then the young dog seemed to relax, her legs and body flattening out against the ground and her head lolling sideways.

"That's better," Fisher said. He glanced at Molly. "Let's get her wrapped up warmly. She's definitely got hypothermia."

Molly pulled a crackly metallic blanket from the pile she'd carried down the slope. She unfolded it and spread it on the ground beside the puppy. Gently, she and Fisher rolled the pup onto it, taking care not to jar her injured leg. They wrapped it around her, then Fisher picked her up carefully.

"It's lucky you guys found her when you did," he said as he started to make his way up the slope, cradling the tiny bundle in his arms. "I'd say she's been here for a couple of days already. Her temperature's dangerously low, and I don't think she'd have lasted another night."

Andi's heart sank. She couldn't bear to think of the puppy lying here, cold and in pain, for two long days and nights. She picked up the spare blankets, Molly grabbed Fisher's medical kit, and they headed back to the sidewalk. Tristan squelched along behind with Natalie and the dogs.

They reached the ASPCA ambulance — a low, white van with neat racks of equipment along one inside wall and a roomy cage to transport stray or injured animals on the other side. Andi flung open the back doors, and Molly climbed in. Fisher laid the puppy in her lap. "I won't put her in the cage. I need you to keep checking her breathing and heartbeat."

Andi reached in and touched the muddy fur. "Hang in there, girl," she said. "You can do it!" She straightened up, and Fisher shut the back door.

"I'm afraid I don't have time to give you three a lift," he said. "But come into the clinic and visit the puppy anytime you want. That was good work, what you did for this little dog today." He smiled briefly, then raced to the driver's door, jumped in, and sped away.

The Pet Finders watched the ambulance until it disappeared around a bend. "I hope she makes it," Tristan said shakily.

"Me, too," Andi and Natalie said together.

"This isn't exactly the sort of pet finding we're used to," Natalie said grimly. "We've never had to cope with an *injured* pet before." She handed Buddy's leash to Andi. "It feels horrible. There's none of the usual energy we get with a new case."

"It was bound to happen one day," Tristan pointed out. "I mean, lost animals must be more at risk of being hit by a car because they've got nobody with them to keep them safe."

Andi nodded, but she was too choked up to say anything. She hugged Buddy tight, thankful that he hadn't been injured when he was lost. Then she wished even harder for the Labrador puppy to pull through.

Chapter Two

"I wonder if anyone's reported the puppy lost," Andi said as the Pet Finders headed for home. Tristan trudged beside them, carrying his skateboard and smelling like the bottom of a pond. "I mean, we haven't heard anything, and most people know who we are now. . . ."

"I was thinking about that, too," Natalie said. "You can't exactly miss the fact that your puppy's not there anymore. They're pretty noticeable!"

Andi thought back to the time when she'd first gotten Buddy. He'd followed her everywhere and was end-lessly setting little presents at her feet — her mom's shoes, newspapers, cushions . . . once he even dug up a small rosebush and dragged it indoors. "Yes," she agreed. "You'd definitely notice if your puppy disappeared."

"I think she's been dumped," Tristan said gloomily.

Andi and Natalie stopped walking. "No way!" Andi exclaimed. "That's too cruel!"

Natalie shook her head. "You're wrong, Tris. Puppies are adorable — especially Labrador puppies." She bent down to hug Jet, and he licked her nose. "Nobody could be that horrible."

"She was on the busiest street in Orchard Park." Tristan shifted his skateboard to the other arm, releasing another whiff of pond scent. "Dogs don't like traffic, so even if she was lost, she'd have turned back when she came to the highway." He set his mouth in a straight line.

"I think you're wrong about this, Tris," Natalie argued.

Andi frowned. What Tristan said made sense, but she couldn't believe that anyone would be cruel enough to abandon a young puppy on a busy highway.

"If she's only lost, then why hasn't her owner reported her missing?" Tristan pointed out. "Fisher and Molly didn't say anything about a missing Labrador puppy, so I guess nobody's called the ASPCA, either."

"Maybe her owners didn't think to call there," Natalie said. "Maybe they called the police instead. We should call the department to find out."

"Good idea," Andi agreed.

The Pet Finders cut across the park. Red-and-white tulips marched along the edge of the grass, and the trees rustled their new leaves. The sun was just dipping behind the mountains on the horizon, and the shadows were lengthening.

Andi let Buddy off his leash. He went tearing away, then circled back as though the kids were a flock of sheep to be rounded up. She envied him for being happy when she couldn't stop thinking about the poor puppy.

Jet looked hopefully at Natalie. "No way!" she said. "I am *not* letting you off your leash, Jet. You wouldn't stay with us like Buddy does." She released the catch on his extendable leash, and he trotted away while the leash unreeled behind him. A few ducks swam toward them, quacking for bread. Buddy raced to the water's edge and barked, his stumpy little tail stuck straight out behind him.

"Do you think it would be okay to call Fisher as soon as we get home, to find out how the puppy's doing?" Andi asked.

"Not right away," Tristan warned. "We don't want to interrupt him or Molly while they're treating the puppy. One of us should call the police, though, like Natalie said."

"I'll do it," Andi offered.

"Let us know what they say," Natalie said. "If they don't know anything about her, we should start searching for her owner. After all, we found a stray owner before, didn't we?" Andi was reminded of Apple, the Border terrier they'd found running in the park a few months earlier.

They reached a narrow path that led out to the street. Andi clipped on Buddy's leash. "I'll call you later," she promised Natalie and Tristan. As she jogged away with Buddy scampering beside her, she tried to feel more positive about the injured puppy. They'd found lost owners before — why not aim for another happy reunion?

Judy Talbot was cooking dinner when Andi got home, and the house smelled delicious. "Hi, honey. Have a good walk?" her mom asked, pulling some potatoes from a grocery bag.

"Not exactly," Andi called back. "Stay, Bud." Buddy sat down obediently on the doormat and watched Andi as she hung up her muddy jacket and grabbed his special towel from the hall cupboard.

"What happened?" Mrs. Talbot asked, appearing in the kitchen doorway with a half-peeled potato in her hand.

Andi started to dry Buddy's muddy paws, but he

made it tricky by catching the towel in his teeth and trying to yank it away from her. She told her mom about
the injured puppy. "Fisher's trying to fix her up now,"
she said. Her voice shook. "Oh, Mom, I'm not sure she's
going to make it."

Her mom came over and gave her a hug. "That poor
little puppy! Still, it sounds as though she's a fighter.
She's held on until now, so she must be strong."

"I wish we'd found her earlier."

"It's lucky you found her at all, sweetheart. Good
for Tris, falling off his skateboard in exactly the right
place!"

Andi nodded. She'd thought about that on her way
home. If Tristan hadn't wanted to practice skateboard
jumps, if he hadn't fallen into the ditch, if Buddy hadn't
found the puppy . . . She shivered. "Can I call the police
and see if anyone's reported her missing?"

"Sure, hon." Mrs. Talbot let her go, then gave her an
encouraging smile. "Are you okay now?"

Andi smiled back. "Yeah, thanks."

"In that case, I'll be in the kitchen if you need me."

Andi dialed the number for the police station. An offi-
cer answered on the third ring.

"Hello. My name's Andi Talbot. My friends and I found
an injured puppy near the highway earlier today," she

explained. "It's a Labrador. Has anyone reported losing one?"

"Just a moment, Andi, I'll check the lost-pet register."

Andi heard him flicking through pages, then he spoke again: "Sorry, no one's lost a Labrador puppy. Have you called the ASPCA?"

"Yes, she's there already," Andi told him. "We called Fisher Pearce, who's a friend of ours, and he picked her up in the ambulance."

"Sounds like you've done this before," the policeman said, sounding impressed.

"Yes. My friends and I are the Pet Finders Club. We track down lost pets — or, sometimes, lost owners."

"I've heard about you," the policeman said. "You found the animals that were stolen from Paws for Thought, didn't you?"

"Right," Andi said. "But nobody's called us about losing a Labrador puppy."

"Give me your phone number," the policeman said. "I'll call if I hear anything. And if you need to call us again, ask for me. I'm Sergeant Poole."

Andi gave him her number. "Thanks for your help." Just as she hung up the phone, it rang again. She snatched it up, hoping it was information about the Lab. "Hello?"

"Is this the Pet Finders Club?" asked a woman's voice.

"Yes! Can I help you?" Andi picked up the pen that lay beside the phone.

"My name's Mrs. Jupp. My son's guinea pig, Cocoa, has disappeared."

Andi felt a twinge of disappointment that the call wasn't about the puppy. Still, it would be good to have another case to work on, too. "Okay. We'll need to get some details." She wrote down the woman's name and address. "We can come over in about half an hour, if that's good for you." Fisher had Natalie's cell phone number, so they wouldn't need to stay home waiting for news of the puppy.

When Mrs. Jupp said that would be fine, Andi called Tristan and Natalie to tell them about the missing guinea pig, then went into the kitchen. Her mom was chopping carrots. "Any update?"

"No. Someone's lost a guinea pig. I've got to go out again. What time's dinner?"

Her mom glanced at the clock. "Not for another hour and a half."

"Okay. I'm only going to Cooper's Hill. Natalie and Tristan are meeting me there. I'll take Rocky's bike so I'll be extra fast." Rocky Brand, the local grocery store owner, had loaned Andi a top-of-the-line mountain bike so she could keep up with Natalie and Tristan.

Buddy darted into the hall as Andi grabbed her coat. "Not this time, Bud," she said. "I'm not sure you'd be too helpful on a guinea-pig hunt." She patted him, then hurried out of the front door leaving him gazing mournfully after her.

The sun was setting in a blaze of crimson and pink as Andi pedaled up Cooper's Hill. Mrs. Jupp's house stood near the top, and Andi grinned to herself. On another one of their recent cases, a missing Dalmatian named Raisin had owners who lived at the top of a hill. Natalie wasn't into sports like Andi was, and she'd complained bitterly about trekking up and down the hill to speak to Mr. and Mrs. Harris on a regular basis.

The Jupps' house was colonial style, with white siding and shuttered windows. There was a kid's bike lying in the front yard. Andi was the first to arrive, but Tristan and Natalie weren't far behind her. Tristan had obviously taken a shower and changed his clothes — there wasn't a trace of mud on him now.

"Any news about the puppy?" Andi asked at once.

"Not yet," Natalie said. "Did you call the police?"

"Yes, but they didn't know anything."

"Told you she'd been dumped," Tristan said darkly.

Natalie sighed. "You don't know what you're talking about, Tristan. There's no way — "

"Whoa, hold on!" Andi interrupted. "We're here to find a lost guinea pig, not to argue about what might have happened to the puppy."

As they walked up Mrs. Jupp's driveway, the front door opened and a dark-haired boy about six years old came out onto the porch. "Are you the Pet Finders Club?"

"Yep," Andi replied. "Is your mom in?"

A tall woman appeared behind the boy. "Hi! Come in," she said, smiling warmly. "I'm Mrs. Jupp."

"I'm Tristan Saunders," Tristan said, as they followed her along a wide hall. "And these are the other Pet Finders, Andi Talbot and Natalie Lewis."

"Pleased to meet you." Mrs. Jupp showed them into a living room cluttered with toys. "It was nice of you to come so quickly."

"So, what happened?" Natalie asked. "If we know how your guinea pig was lost, it might help us figure out where to look."

"It was Shane who discovered she was missing," Mrs. Jupp replied. "Tell them what happened, honey."

"Cocoa was in her hutch in the yard, with her friend Sugar — " the little boy explained, his forehead creasing with worry. "When I went out to feed them, Sugar was there, but Cocoa wasn't."

"Had the door of the hutch come open?" asked Andi.

Shane shook his head. "No, it was shut. I don't know how she got out."

Tristan took notes in the small red binder he used for every case. "When did you notice she was missing?"

"Just before Mom called you. We came back from shopping. Mom said we should call because it's such a mystery how she got out."

"Can we see the hutch?" Natalie suggested.

Mrs. Jupp opened a pair of French doors at the back of the living room, and they went out into a small yard. The sun had almost gone down now, and the garden was full of deep shadows. A neat wooden hutch stood at the end of the lawn, next to a shed. A white guinea pig was sitting inside the hutch, nibbling hay. A path led past the hutch to a gate at the back of the yard.

"The guinea pigs live outside in spring and summer," Mrs. Jupp explained. "They love to sunbathe."

"Maybe the hinge is broken on the door of the hutch," Andi whispered, remembering how Lola, a valuable Russian Blue cat, had escaped from her owner's home.

Tristan nodded. "Like Lola, you mean?" he said, reading her mind. "Good idea. Let's check it out."

"Hello. You must be Sugar. Aren't you sweet?" Natalie said to the guinea pig as she unbolted the door. The guinea pig gazed up at her, its nose twitching.

"Don't be scared, Sugar," Shane said, crouching beside the hutch. "They're here to find Cocoa."

The guinea pig gave a high-pitched squeak before scampering into its sleeping compartment.

Tristan laughed. "I always thought you looked scary, Nat."

Natalie made a face at him, then examined the door. "The hinges are fine," she announced. "And the wire mesh is tight. There's no way Cocoa could have gotten through here."

"Unless the door wasn't closed right," Andi said. She rattled the bolt, but it fit well and slid easily into place. As she checked the door to the sleeping compartment, Sugar dashed back into the main part of her hutch. "This door's okay, too." She reached into the hutch very slowly and pet the guinea pig with one finger, trying to calm her. "It's okay, we won't hurt you."

"Do Sugar and Cocoa look alike, Mrs. Jupp?" Tristan asked.

"Oh, no. Cocoa's chocolate brown."

"I've got a picture of her by my bed," Shane said. "Wanna see it?"

"That would be great!" Tristan agreed.

Shane hurried inside.

Andi and Natalie closed the hutch, checking that the bolts were securely in place, then went to examine the back gate. It wasn't locked, and Tristan opened it to reveal a narrow alley that ran behind all the houses on the street. The gate had no gaps around it, so the guinea pig couldn't have escaped that way.

Tristan drew a quick sketch of the gate in his notebook.

"Honestly, Tris, we all know what a gate looks like!" Natalie exclaimed.

He grinned sheepishly and crossed it out. "I guess so."

Shane came back clutching the photo. "This is her."

Andi took the photo, which was in a red-and-green frame. "She looks really cute. Do you think we could keep this for a while? We need to scan it into my computer and make posters asking people to look out for Cocoa."

Shane bit his lip. "You won't lose it, will you? It's the only one I've got." He looked as though he was about to cry. "Sugar is great," he added, "but Cocoa's my real favorite."

"We'll be really careful with it," Andi promised. "Look, Tristan's got a special pouch in his notebook for photos."

Tristan slid the photo out of the frame and put it inside the clear plastic pouch. "It'll be safe there."

Shane looked a little happier as he took back the empty frame. "Are you going to make the posters now?"

"It'll have to be tomorrow. It's getting late," Andi replied. "And we need to search for Cocoa in your yard, but it's too dark now."

"We've already searched our yard and garden," Mrs. Jupp said. "She's definitely not here."

Andi frowned. "I don't see how she could have gotten out of the yard."

"Well, actually, the gate was open," said Shane.

"Are you sure, honey?" asked Mrs. Jupp, looking surprised. "You didn't mention it before."

The little boy opened his eyes very wide. "I just remembered, but it *was* open."

"So she might have gone out into the alley," Tristan said. He lowered his voice. "Do you think someone came in through the gate and stole her?"

"Maybe," Natalie replied. "But it would be pretty mean to steal a little kid's pet. It's more likely she just wandered out of the yard."

"You *are* going to find her, aren't you?" Shane's voice quivered.

Andi smiled, trying to reassure him. "We'll do every-thing we can. Don't worry — we haven't been beaten yet!"

All the same, she couldn't help feeling anxious. There were so many dangers facing a little lost guinea pig. She hoped Cocoa would find somewhere safe to hide.

Chapter Three

The next day after school, the Pet Finders hurried to the ASPCA. Fisher was sitting in the reception area going through a pile of forms.

"How's the puppy?" Andi asked right away. Fisher had called Natalie on her cell phone the night before to say that the pup was still alive, but Andi had hardly been able to concentrate at school, wondering constantly how she was doing.

Fisher stood up and smiled. "She's going to be fine! We X-rayed her and, luckily, she's got no broken bones or internal injuries."

"What about the hypothermia?" Natalie wanted to know.

"Her temperature's back to normal, thanks to a warm drip. Molly took it out about fifteen minutes ago."

"And her dislocated hip?" said Tristan.

"It's back in place. She's still a bit dopey from the anesthetic, but that's a good thing because she needs to rest. Aside from that, she's bruised and she's got a couple of minor cuts. She'll be a little stiff and sore for a few days, but she'll make a full recovery."

Andi high-fived Natalie and Tristan. The puppy was going to get better! It was the best news ever! "Can we see her?"

"Sure, you can," Fisher said. "I'll take you through." He led them into a large room filled with pens and cages of different sizes. Molly was scrubbing down a counter at the far end of the room, but she looked around and smiled at them. "Hi! Did Fisher tell you the good news?"

The Pet Finders grinned back. "You bet!" Tristan exclaimed. "And it's — " He broke off and his eyes stretched wide with delight. "Wow! Look at these geckos!" He darted to a cage containing a pair of green geckos and a branch for them to climb on. The geckos gazed at him, their yellow eyes unblinking and their tongues flicking in and out.

"Trust you to make a beeline for them," Natalie said. She crouched down beside a cage with a low wooden hutch at one end. "These guys are much cuter." There were five fluffy, white, baby rabbits scampering about in the sawdust. The biggest rabbit — the babies' mother,

Andi guessed — was nibbling a carrot, but she stopped chewing and sat up on her hind legs as they bent down. One of the babies came cautiously to the wire, its pink nose snuffling. Andi pushed her fingers through and stroked its downy fur.

Suddenly, they heard a high-pitched shout. "Ahoy there!" The baby rabbits skittered back to their mother.

"What was that?" Andi gasped.

Fisher laughed. "It's only Captain." He pointed to a green-and-red parrot that was strutting along its perch in a tall cage. "Time for lunch! Lovely!" it screeched. "Lovely! Lovely!"

The Pet Finders laughed. "He's almost as loud as Long John Silver," Natalie said.

"Who?" Molly looked puzzled.

"Fisher's mom and dad have a parrot," Andi explained. "They own the Banana Beach Café on Main Street. Long John Silver seems to spend most of his time squawking about bananas."

Molly grinned. "I look forward to meeting him."

"Are all these animals lost?" Tristan asked. From the way he said it, Andi knew he was hoping Fisher would let them track down the owners.

Fisher shook his head. "No, the rabbits were left on our doorstep one night. The geckos' owner found that looking after them was too much trouble. And Captain's owner was an old lady who's gone to live in a home. None of them will be here long. We'll find new homes for them. We've already placed two cats and a hamster this month."

Tristan looked longingly at the geckos. "Can anyone have them?"

"No. We check out prospective owners first, to make sure they're responsible."

"That leaves you out, Tris," Natalie whispered.

"Whatever," Tristan retorted.

"You have Lucy to look after now, anyway," Andi added. "You'd never have time for geckos, too." Tristan's cat, Lucy, had been missing for months until the Pet Finders had recently tracked her down.

Tristan beamed at her. "You don't have to remind me. Having Lucy home is *fantastic*!"

"The puppy's through here," Fisher said. He led them to a door at the end of the room. "This is the intensive care room. She should be well enough to move into the main room tomorrow."

The cages in the intensive care room were smaller, and only one was occupied. The Pet Finders crowded around. The puppy was lying inside on a white blanket. She was a lot cleaner than she had been when they found her, though streaks of dried mud still clung to her fur.

"She's a *golden* Lab!" Tristan exclaimed. "She was so muddy yesterday it was impossible to tell."

"She wasn't the only one!" Natalie grinned at Tristan.

The puppy had a small cut on one leg and another just below her ear, but they obviously didn't bother her too much. Her tail began to wag the moment she saw the Pet Finders, and she struggled to sit up.

"Hey, girl!" Andi whispered. Her heart was zinging with happiness. Only yesterday, she'd been afraid the puppy wouldn't last the night, but now she seemed to be making a miraculous recovery. And she was *so* gorgeous! Andi pushed her fingers through the mesh of the cage, and the puppy licked them.

"We should think of a name for her," Natalie suggested. "You know, like we called that Border terrier Oat until we found out her real name was Apple. We can't keep calling her *the puppy*." She frowned thoughtfully. "How about Goldie?"

"Not very original," Andi pointed out. "After everything she's been through, she needs an extra-special name." She rubbed the side of the pup's head, trying to think of a name to suit her, but nothing seemed right.

"We have to hurry up and find her owner now,"

Natalie said, reaching in to run a velvety ear through her fingers. "They must be so worried about her."

"Absolutely," Fisher agreed. "But I'm sure you Pet Finders will find out where she's from."

"I think she's been dumped," Tristan said. "Could she have been pushed out of a moving car, do you think?"

Andi gasped. "Oh, no! Nobody could have done that to her, Tris!"

Fisher shook his head. "No. She's only bruised on one side of her body, and that must have happened when she was hit by a car. Luckily, it was only a light blow. If she'd been pushed out of a moving car, I think she'd have been hurt much worse. I'd expect to find two distinct areas of bruising, one from the fall and the other from the impact with the car."

Andi was relieved that Tristan's theory seemed to be wrong but, all the same, it made her shiver. She could imagine the little dog's terror as she went bowling down the steep bank, knocked off her paws by a passing vehicle.

"If she hasn't been dumped, why hasn't anybody reported her missing?" Tristan persisted. "And why was she on that busy road at all? She wouldn't have gone there by herself, with all that traffic rushing past."

"It does seem a little odd," Fisher agreed, "but it's not

cut and dried. It's important to find the puppy's owner, but we should be wary. We don't want her going home to someone who's not fit to look after her. On the other hand, maybe there's an innocent explanation for everything."

Andi's head was reeling. She still couldn't understand how anyone would abandon such a cute puppy. But if she hadn't been dumped, why hadn't anyone reported her missing? Andi felt torn in two directions at once. All she knew for sure was that the puppy needed their help, and the Pet Finders were going to have to do everything they could to make sure she ended up with someone who really cared about her.

Chapter Four

"Let's make Cocoa's posters first," Andi suggested, sitting down at the computer in her mom's study. Buddy flopped down under the desk and rested his head on her feet. "We've got everything we need for those," she continued. "We don't have a photo of the puppy yet, and it might be better to wait until her cuts have healed a little before we start taking pictures of her."

"And the puppy's safe at the ASPCA," Tristan pointed out. "But the guinea pig's in danger while she's on the loose." He perched on the edge of the desk and took the red binder out of his backpack. Removing Cocoa's photo from the pouch, he handed it to Andi. "Here you go."

She scanned it into the computer, then typed Lost underneath, to begin with.

"We can ask people to look under bushes and in

sheds," Tristan said. "And they should check under parked cars and — "

"Okay, okay, slow down!" Andi exclaimed. "I'm not *that* fast at typing."

The poster was soon finished. Andi printed off a trial copy and passed it around. "What do you think?"

"Not bad," Tristan said approvingly. "Let's hope it works. I hate to think of Cocoa scampering around all alone." Andi printed twenty more copies, then she reduced the size of the poster and printed thirty flyers to put in mailboxes on the Jupps' street.

Andi glanced out of the window and saw that it was raining. "We should meet in the morning and hang these up before school," she suggested.

"Uh, what time in the morning?" Natalie asked suspiciously.

"Seven o'clock."

"Seven o'clock? No, thanks!"

"You've got to come, Nat. We're the Pet Finders. We do stuff together. And this case is urgent."

"Yeah, but seven o'clock?"

"And we should run there," Andi continued, "so we can get in shape at the same time."

"Run!" Natalie sank back into her chair. "You're crazy."

"Completely insane," Tristan agreed.

"It's track season," Andi reminded them. "I should be running every day." Andi loved track, and tryouts were coming up for the school team.

"Can't we use our bikes?" Natalie said. "Tristan could come on his skateboard."

Tristan frowned. "Actually, I can't. One of the bearings broke when I fell." He dropped the red notebook into his backpack and stood up. "And I can't borrow Dean's because he'll be delivering his papers. I hate to say it, but I think Andi's right. We *will* have to run. What luck!"

"We'll meet outside the school. Don't forget to wear your sneakers, Nat," Andi said, giving her friend a playful jab on her arm.

Natalie groaned and waved Andi away with her hand.

"Well, I'd better get home," Tristan said. "I've got a pile of homework the size of Mount Everest."

"I can't believe we're going to do this," Natalie said as she followed Tristan downstairs. "I mean . . . running! And at seven o'clock in the morning."

Andi laughed. "See you then," she said as Tristan and Natalie put up their hoods and went out into the rain.

The next morning, the sun was shining and the sky was clear blue. Andi ran to Fairfield Middle School with

Buddy scampering happily beside her. There was nothing he liked better than an early run.

Tristan was already there. "Do you think Nat will show up?"

Andi looked down the street. "Here she comes now. And she brought Jet."

Natalie was pounding determinedly along the sidewalk, wearing a spotless white T-shirt, pink Lycra shorts, and silver sneakers that gleamed in the early morning sunshine. "Typical," Andi said as Natalie reached them.

Buddy and Jet touched noses, then danced around each other. Jet began to bark. "We'd better go," Andi said. "We have to leave enough time to get home again before school, and we don't want to wake people up. It's early."

"You can say that again," Natalie muttered.

They set off jogging. At first, Tristan tried to keep pace with Andi, while Natalie puffed along behind. But soon he fell back, and by the time they reached the end of the street, quite a gap had opened up between them. Andi waited for them to catch up. "Come on!" she called, running on the spot.

"I don't know why I came," Natalie panted when she reached Andi. "I knew this would be a disaster." She hunched over with her hands on her knees. Jet leaped around her, pulling on his leash. "Stop it, Jet!" She groaned. "It's too early to play."

"Next time I mention running," Tristan panted, sinking down on a garden wall, "would someone please remind me that I'm a natural-born couch potato?"

"Think of all the good it's doing you," Andi said, but she could tell neither of them was convinced. "And think of poor Cocoa."

"I know, I know," Natalie said, "but I just need a minute to get my breath back."

"I'll go on ahead, or we won't have time to put any of these posters up," Andi said, and she set off at a sprint.

"Slow down!" Natalie wailed.

Cooper's Hill was only a block away, but by the time Andi reached the corner, Tristan and Natalie were a long way behind. "I don't know, Bud," she laughed, stooping down to pet him. "Some people never get any exercise!" She took the posters out of her backpack and tied one to a tree. Cocoa's cute face stared back at her. "I hope these do the trick," she said aloud.

Tristan and Natalie arrived at last, red-faced and out of breath. Andi divided up the pile of posters and flyers and handed them out, keeping one poster for the school bulletin board and another to hang in the window of Paws for Thought, Christine Wilson's pet shop.

"Here," Andi said. "If we get a move on, there should just be time for a quick look along the street before we have to head back."

Natalie glanced at the steep hill ahead of them and shuddered.

"It's okay," Andi said. "Bud and I will go up the hill. You and Tris can start down here."

Soon every tree and lamppost on Cooper's Hill and the roads around it displayed a lost guinea-pig poster, and every mailbox contained a flyer. The Pet Finders met halfway up the hill. Tristan and Natalie had recovered from their run now, though Natalie's face was still red and shiny.

"Let's start searching in the alley behind the Jupps' house," Tristan suggested. "That's the most likely place for Cocoa to be. She could have escaped through the back gate. And she'd try to keep herself hidden in case there were any predators around."

They found a narrow passageway between two houses that looked like it might lead into the alley. It was obviously not used much — they had to push their way through tall weeds and drooping branches that hung over from the yards on either side. They scanned the ground among the weeds carefully. It was just the sort of place a lost and frightened guinea pig might hide. But they reached the alley without seeing any sign of Cocoa.

The alley ran straight in both directions. It was rutted and stony, with tufts of coarse grass. Several houses had garages here, and a few trash cans stood beside back gates.

"Let's head up the hill toward the Jupps'," Natalie suggested. They turned left and continued their search, standing on tiptoe to look over fences, peering behind trash cans and into clumps of thick grass.

"We should look for gnawed places on fences, too," Tristan said. "Guinea pigs nibble wood to keep their teeth from getting too long, so if we found bite marks we'd know Cocoa had been there."

Just before they reached the Jupps' house, Andi glanced at her watch. It was quarter to eight. "We'd better stop. We'll be late for school."

As they headed back down the alley, Tristan sighed. "Guinea pigs are so small and vulnerable. . . ." He didn't finish, but Andi knew exactly what he meant. Cocoa would be no match for a hungry cat or raccoon. The thought made her shiver. They had to find the guinea pig quickly. If it wasn't already too late. . . .

Chapter Five

The Pet Finders walked to the ASPCA after school to pay another visit to the Labrador puppy. Molly was sitting in the reception area. She was holding a milk dropper in one hand and a pink, featherless baby bird in the other. Its beak kept opening and shutting, and it was chirping loudly.

The Pet Finders crept closer, not wanting to frighten it. "Where did you get the baby bird?" Andi whispered.

Molly dripped milk into the tiny beak. "Someone brought it in. It fell out of its nest."

"How's the dog with no name?" Natalie asked.

"See for yourself!" Smiling, Molly set down the dropper and, ignoring the baby bird's insistent chirps, opened the door that led into the animal unit. The puppy was curled up in a cage near the door. She lifted her head as they approached, then pushed herself to her paws. They all bent down and reached through the mesh. The puppy licked their fingers, her tail wagging the tiniest bit.

"She's still a little muddy, I'm afraid," Molly said. "I've been trying to find time to bathe her all day, but it's been really hectic here."

"Can we let her out?" said Natalie.

"Yeah, though I don't think she'll feel much like running. She's still pretty stiff."

"Her cuts look like they're healing," Tristan remarked.

"They are. Her temperature's normal, too, and that hip's as good as new."

The Pet Finders opened the cage door. The puppy came toward them slowly, her tail twitching from side to side. "Hello, girl. How are you feeling?" Andi murmured, bending down to stroke her.

When Tristan sat cross-legged on the floor, the puppy crawled onto his lap and snuggled down. Now they could see the flecks of dried mud still caught in her fur.

"She's so gorgeous," Natalie said, smoothing the platinum fur on the top of the pup's head. "We really can't keep on calling her 'the dog with no name.' We've got to think of a temporary name for her."

"It's so difficult," Andi said. "There are tons of names that would fit her. How can we pick the right one?"

They sat silent for a few moments, thinking hard. "I give up. Let's think about something else," Tristan said. "You know, Molly said she hasn't had time to give her a bath. So, why don't *we* do it?"

"Do you think they'll let us?" Natalie asked eagerly.

"Only one way to find out." Andi stood up and went back to reception. The baby bird was asleep in a plastic bowl lined with newspaper. It didn't look as comfy as a nest, but it was a lot safer than being on a sidewalk. Molly was washing her hands in a sink at the far end of the room.

"We were wondering if we could give the puppy a bath," Andi said. "We'll be really careful with her."

Molly smiled over her shoulder. "That would be a big help. I'll give you a hand filling the tub." She got a plastic tub out of a walk-in closet and carried it to the sink. Andi squirted a dollop of dog shampoo into the tub and turned on the tap. The shampoo began to foam.

"That should do it," Molly said when the tub was almost full. She tested the temperature of the water with her hand. "Perfect." She threw a soft, white towel over her shoulder.

They carefully lifted the heavy tub together, and shuffled along with small side steps, back to the animal unit. The bubbles shimmered with rainbows of color as they set the tub down. The puppy looked up and sniffed the air, her round, black nose quivering. Then she stood up on Tristan's lap and stretched gingerly.

"Come on, girl!" Andi called as she and Molly kneeled down by the tub. "Bath time."

The puppy padded toward her, her thick, soft ears perked up and her brown eyes bright. Tristan and Natalie followed.

"You'll have to ruffle her fur a little to get the mud off her skin," Molly said. She handed the towel to Natalie. "Labs have two layers of hair, and the undercoat is waterproof."

"Waterproof?" Natalie echoed. "Why would a dog need a waterproof coat?"

"Labradors are good swimmers," Molly explained. "Fishermen in Newfoundland used to keep Labs to help them drag their nets out of the water."

"That must be how she stayed warm enough to survive when she fell in the ditch," Andi said thoughtfully.

"Well, I'll leave you to it," said Molly. "Shout if you need me."

"Is it okay to lift her?" Natalie checked. "We don't want to hurt her."

"I'm sure you'll be gentle," Molly replied. "Just don't rub too hard when you're washing her."

"Do you think she likes baths?" Natalie wondered when Molly had gone. "Jet is terrible in the tub. He always acts up."

"Buddy loves baths," Andi said. "Let's hope this puppy's more like he is." She lifted the pup carefully and set her down in the warm water. The little Labrador looked down at the foam for a moment, then flopped down so that only her head was above the water. The bubbles around her neck made it look as though she was wearing a lacy ruff.

"Good girl!" Andi laughed. She scooped up a handful of water and let it trickle over the puppy's fluffy ears. The little Labrador gave a tiny yap, as if to tell them to do it again.

"She loves this," Tristan said, crouching down to rub her back.

The puppy dipped her nose into the bubbles and sneezed. She stared around at the Pet Finders, wide-eyed with surprise. They all laughed and the puppy's tail wagged harder, flicking bubbles over them. "You're right, Tris," Andi agreed. "She *does* like it!"

Andi and Tristan washed the puppy carefully, working

the soap bubbles through her fur to clean away the last of the mud, while Natalie spread the towel over her lap, ready to dry her. "We still haven't thought of a name for her," she reminded them.

"I've got one," Tristan said with a grin. "How about Fang?"

"Fang!" Natalie hooted. "Does this sweet little dog look like a Fang? And, in any case, her owner would never have called her a name like that."

"How about Ripper, then?" Tristan suggested. "If she has a really tough-sounding name, she'll be able to stick up for herself if other dogs try to bully her."

"Yeah, like that would work!" Natalie retorted.

"Demon?" Tristan said. "Or — "

"Okay, Tris," Andi interrupted. "Don't get carried away." She wiped bubbles from the puppy's head. "You don't want a fierce name, do you, girl?"

The puppy twisted her head and licked Andi's hand. "There's your answer, Tris," Andi joked. "She doesn't think much of your ideas. And neither do we."

"You're only saying that because you didn't think of them yourself," Tristan said, pretending to be offended. "Fang's a great name. We could get her a studded collar and . . ."

"No way!" Andi and Natalie said together.

"I think we're about done here," Andi said. "Let's get you out of there, girl." She lifted the puppy out of the bath and set her on Natalie's lap. Natalie wrapped her in the towel and patted her gently. The dog leaned against her chest, grunting with pleasure.

Andi and Tristan hauled the tub back to the sink and emptied it. Andi rinsed it and wiped it dry, then returned it to the closet. By the time they got back, Natalie had finished drying the puppy. Her damp fur stood up in golden spikes all over her body.

"That's better," Natalie said and set her down on the floor. She tried to smooth down her fur. "Maybe we should call her Spike."

"Too boyish," Andi said, wrinkling her nose.

The puppy walked in a rather wobbly circle. "She doesn't look so stiff anymore," Tristan said. "That warm water must have helped with her aches and pains."

Andi shook out the puppy's blanket and refolded it to get rid of any uncomfortable creases. "There you go, girl."

The puppy padded into the cage, then settled down in her basket with her head on her paws. In a few moments she was fast asleep — it seemed like taking a bath was tiring work.

"We should go," Natalie said. "We've still got to find

Shane's guinea pig, and we need to work on finding the puppy's owner."

Fisher came into the room. "Hey, guys," he said. "The puppy's looking good, isn't she?"

"Great!" Tristan agreed. "Can we bring her a bone as a treat?"

"Actually, bones are still too hard for her teeth. She's only about ten weeks old."

"How about corn?" Andi suggested. "Corn on the cob, I mean. Buddy was crazy about it when he was little."

"Corncobs?" asked Natalie.

"That's a good idea, Andi," Fisher said enthusiastically. "I've never heard of a dog eating corn on the cob, but it sounds perfect. Crunchy for puppy teeth, but soft enough for young gums."

"So it's okay if we come and see her again?" Tristan said.

"Of course. Anyone can visit. The more contact she has with people, the more social skills she'll learn. We don't want her to turn into a loner when she's still so young. It'll keep her from getting bored, too, if she has plenty of visitors."

The Pet Finders went out into the sunshine. "Let's get Buddy and Jet and go down to Paws for Thought,"

Tristan suggested. "We can ask Christine if she knows of anyone who's lost a Labrador puppy or found a missing guinea pig. We can't forget we have two cases to solve right now."

As the Pet Finders headed for Paws for Thought with Buddy and Jet trotting beside them, they heard the sound of rapid footsteps. A moment later, Mike Morgan, the mailman, came sprinting around the corner. He was tall and lean with black dreadlocked hair tied back in a ponytail.

Jet raced over to say hello, his extendable leash unreeling and his tail wagging furiously. Buddy ran close behind, yanking Andi after him. The mailman staggered back with a startled yell.

"Don't worry, Mike!" said Andi, pulling Jet and Buddy back.

"O-okay." Mike eyed the dogs anxiously.

Andi noticed that his hand was bandaged. "What happened to your hand?"

"A German shepherd bit me last week." He shook his head. "I didn't see it until I was halfway up the driveway with a package, but it had been lying down in the shade. Chased me all the way to the gate! I'd have gotten away, too, if the catch on the gate hadn't been so stiff." He sighed melodramatically. "Dogs just do *not* like mailmen!"

"Maybe not all of them," Natalie said, "but Jet's friendly with everyone!"

"So's Buddy," Andi added.

"I won't test them on that, if you don't mind." Mike edged away from the dogs as he spoke, then took a package out of his bag and looked down at it, his forehead creasing in a frown.

"Is everything okay?" asked Tristan.

Mike shrugged. "Sure. It's just that I've got this box to deliver." He glanced nervously across the road. "There's a really big dog at this address. I haven't seen it, but it always barks when I ring the doorbell. I try to leave all the mail in the mailbox, but this box is just too big. I'll have to take it to the door and, with my luck, the dog will burst out the moment someone answers the bell."

"I'll take it," Andi offered.

The lines in Mike's face smoothed out. "Really?"

"Sure, I don't mind big dogs."

Mike handed her the package, holding it at arm's length, so that Buddy couldn't get too near him. "It's number three, just over there." He pointed to a single-story house with a birdbath in the middle of the front lawn.

Andi checked that no cars were coming, then ran across the street and up the driveway. Buddy scampered beside her, his claws clicking on the concrete. As soon as she pressed the doorbell, a dog inside began to bark. It sounded enormous. Buddy pricked up his ears and put his front paws on the doorstep, ready to make friends. Andi held his leash tightly. She didn't want him diving inside when the door opened — strange dogs could be unpredictable.

To Andi's astonishment, a tiny old lady opened the door. Andi couldn't imagine how she could possibly look after such a big dog; it was a wonder it didn't pull her over when she took it for walks. "Hello, dear," the lady said.

"I have a package for you," Andi explained, handing it over. She peered past the lady, hoping to catch a glimpse of her pet. "Your dog sounds huge."

The lady winked at Andi. She had a very sweet face and twinkling blue eyes. "That's not a dog, dear. It's a tape recording. It switches on automatically when someone presses the doorbell. Don't tell anyone, okay? I feel better with people thinking there's a big, fierce dog living here!"

Andi laughed. "It's scaring away the mailman! Can I tell *him*?"

She thought about it for a moment and then said, "I don't see why not."

Andi crossed back over the road and told Mike what she had learned.

"A recording?" He tutted indignantly. "Honestly! I've been dreading delivering that package, and all the time there wasn't a thing to worry about!" He thanked Andi, said good-bye to the others, and jogged away shaking his head.

Christine's cocker spaniel, Max, was lying in his favorite sunny spot in the window of Paws for Thought. He stood up, wagging his tail, and trotted over to greet them. Andi ran her hand over his silky fur. "Hi, boy!"

Max touched noses with Buddy and Jet.

Christine came out of the storeroom behind the shop. "Hi, there! I thought I heard voices." She had dark curly hair that hung to her shoulders, and she was wearing jeans and a dark green sweatshirt with the Paws For Thought logo — a dog's paw print surrounded by the store name — on the front. "I hear you saved a puppy yesterday."

"You've been talking to Fisher," Tristan deduced.

Christine grinned and held up her hands. "You got me! He popped in yesterday evening."

"We thought you might know someone who owns the puppy," Natalie said. "She's a golden Lab, about ten weeks old."

Christine shook her head. "I know plenty of people with golden Labs, but none as young as that. Still, I'll ask around. Do you want me to put up a poster for her?"

"We haven't made one yet," Andi admitted. "We thought we'd wait until her cuts heal before we take her picture. But we *have* got a guinea-pig poster. Would you mind if we put that up?"

"A lost guinea pig?" Christine said as Natalie stuck the poster in the window. "Hope you have some leads on that one."

"Not really," Tristan confessed. "Has anyone tried to sell you a guinea pig lately?"

"No."

"Or maybe you've had a new customer who's bought guinea-pig food or a book about guinea pigs?"

"No, sorry. " She stopped as a thin-faced man came in carrying a large dog basket. "Hang on, guys," she said. "I need to help this customer."

"Hi," he greeted her, heaving the dog bed onto the counter. "I was wondering if you'd be interested in buying this bed. It's hardly been used at all."

The Pet Finders watched from the other side of the

store. "Poor guy. Do you think his dog died?" Natalie whispered.

"He doesn't look too upset if it did," Tristan pointed out. "But I can't see any other reason why anyone would sell a nearly new dog — " He broke off suddenly, his eyes gleaming. "Unless he got rid of his dog! By dumping it, maybe?"

"Oh, no, Tris," Andi said. "You can't be suggesting he's the puppy's owner."

"He *could* be," Tristan insisted. He moved a little closer to the counter, eyeing the man suspiciously.

"It would be way too much of a coincidence that we're in Christine's store when the puppy's owner shows up trying to sell her bed," Andi whispered, pulling Tristan behind a stand displaying pet toys. "And don't make it so obvious that we're eavesdropping!" She picked up a rubber bone and began to examine it.

"In any case," Natalie added, "I keep telling you, that puppy wasn't dumped. Her owners are probably searching frantically for her right now."

"Yeah, right," Tristan said. "Let's listen to what he's saying," he added hurriedly as Natalie opened her mouth to argue.

"It's in perfect condition," the man said. "My puppy

only used it for a few weeks. She's growing so quickly, she won't fit into it anymore."

"That basket's huge!" Tristan whispered, peering around the pet-toy stand. "His dog must be a monster if it can't fit in there."

"I'm afraid I don't sell used equipment," Christine said. "Sorry."

The man shrugged. "Thanks, anyway," he said, before picking up the dog basket and going out.

Tristan darted to the counter. "Do you know him, Christine?" he demanded. "Is he one of your regular customers?"

"No, I've never seen him before. Why?"

"Tristan thinks he's the puppy's owner," Andi explained.

Christine frowned. "He said his dog had *outgrown* the basket, not that he'd *lost* his dog."

"Yeah, but nobody has a dog too big for a basket that size," Tristan argued.

"Maybe it's a Saint Bernard or a Great Dane," Christine said. "They get pretty big."

"Or, maybe he doesn't need a bed anymore because he dumped his dog on the highway!" Tristan countered.

"But the bed was too big for a puppy," Andi pointed

out. She realized that she was still holding the rubber bone and hung it back on the display stand.

"Lots of people buy beds for their puppies that will be big enough for them when they're fully grown," Christine said. "It's expensive having to buy beds in two different sizes."

"There you are, then!" Tristan exclaimed. He ran to the door and looked along the street.

"Not that I'm agreeing with what Tristan's saying," Christine added. "I'm just giving you the facts."

"The puppy wasn't dumped," Natalie said determinedly. "You're completely wrong about this, Tris. Tell him, Andi!"

But before Andi could say anything, Tristan turned around, his eyes gleaming mischievously. "The guy's looking in the baker's window, just down the block!" he whispered. "Let's follow him and see where he goes."

Chapter Six

Andi cringed. Suppose Tristan was right about the man with the dog basket being the puppy's owner? If they didn't follow him, they could miss out on the chance to solve another case. Though, if the puppy had been abandoned, Andi wasn't sure she even wanted to track down her owner.

"Come on!" Tristan urged, beckoning. "He'll get away if we don't hurry."

"Okay," Andi agreed. "I guess there's no harm in following him. Come on, Nat."

"But . . ." Natalie protested.

Tristan grabbed her arm and marched her outside. Andi followed them, still not sure that they were doing the right thing.

"There he goes!" Tristan hissed. The man was walking slowly along the sidewalk with the basket under his arm.

"Remember the way we suspected all the wrong people when Christine's animals were stolen from Paws for Thought?" Natalie said. "We're making the same mistake again. This guy is not the puppy's owner, I'm sure of it."

"But what if he is, and we let him go?" Andi countered. "I know Tristan jumps to wild conclusions sometimes — "

"I do not!"

Andi ignored him. "But he might be right someday. And what if today's the day? It won't hurt to check the guy out."

"He's acting really suspicious," Tristan insisted. "Puppies don't grow as fast as that."

"His story does sound pretty unlikely," Natalie agreed. "I guess Andi's right. It won't hurt to follow him."

They set off down the sidewalk. Soon the man crossed the road and turned onto a side street. The Pet Finders sped up. Halfway down the street, he stopped by a parked car and rummaged in his pockets.

"Uh-oh. He's going to drive away," Tristan groaned.

The man unlocked his car, placed the dog bed on the passenger seat, and climbed in.

The Pet Finders looked at one another in dismay. "Let's get closer," Tristan urged. "At least I'll be able to memorize the license plate." He began to run, and Andi and Natalie raced after him.

"What good will that do?" Natalie was already short of breath. "We can't track him down with a license plate number. Only the police can do that."

Tristan didn't answer, he just kept running.

The car pulled away as Tristan reached it. "He's heading this way, Nat!" Andi yelled. "Take a picture of him with your cell phone!"

Natalie pulled it out and flipped it open. As the man drove toward her, she snapped his photo. The car had reached them when, suddenly, a huge shaggy dog sat up in the backseat. It was so big, its head touched the ceiling and its tail brushed the window on the other side.

Andi and Natalie gazed openmouthed. "He was telling the truth!" Andi gasped. "His dog really *is* enormous."

Tristan came toward them. "Did you see that?" he said in astonishment. "Was that dog massive or was that dog massive? I bet it eats whole cows for breakfast."

"We need a new lead," Andi noted. "Anyone got any ideas?"

"We should really print some posters of the puppy." Natalie glanced at her watch. "But we're too late to take photos of her today. The ASPCA will be closed."

"Tomorrow, then," Andi decided. "We'll take them right after school."

Andi woke up early the next morning. She opened the curtains and sat on her windowsill in a patch of sunshine, thinking about the Labrador puppy. Fisher had said that she needed lots of visitors to keep her from getting bored, but the Pet Finders still had to find Shane's missing guinea pig, so they couldn't spend as much time with the puppy as Andi would have liked.

Footsteps sounded on the sidewalk outside. Twisting around, she saw Mike the mailman out for an early morning run. Her thoughts switched to the way he had been so nervous to deliver a package to the house where he'd heard a big dog barking.

What he needs is a crash course in getting along with dogs, she thought to herself. And suddenly, she knew just the dog to help him! Buddy! He was small and friendly and very obedient when he was in the right mood. No one could be frightened by him.

"Mike!" she called, leaning out of the window.

The mailman glanced around, surprised.

"Up here!"

Mike looked up at her.

"Hang on!" Andi called. "I have an idea!" She dressed hurriedly and rushed downstairs. Buddy came scampering out of the kitchen, his tail wagging furiously. "No early walk this morning, Bud," Andi told him. She gave him a quick pat, then let herself out the front door.

Mike was waiting on the sidewalk, looking puzzled. "What idea?" He smiled at Andi.

"To cure your fear of dogs!"

His smile vanished. "It doesn't involve me getting close to one, does it?"

"You wouldn't be frightened if you realized how friendly they are," Andi insisted.

Mike gave a hollow laugh. "They're not friendly to me." He held up his bandaged hand. "They're downright vicious."

"Come and meet Buddy. He'll show you that most dogs aren't like that."

"No, thanks."

"Come on, Buddy's so small," Andi said persuasively. "He wouldn't hurt a fly."

Mike pushed back his baseball cap and shrugged. "I guess I could give it a try."

"Great! Come on." Andi led the way back to her house, then raced up the driveway. Mike followed her slowly.

As Andi opened the front door, Buddy came bursting

out. Mike stopped and eyed the little Jack Russell warily as he darted toward him.

"Here, Bud!" Andi called.

Buddy trotted back to her at once, his stumpy tail wagging. Andi grinned with relief. Buddy was obviously in the right mood.

"I'll put him on his leash," she told Mike, clipping it to Buddy's collar. "There. Now, come a little closer."

Mike approached slowly.

"Sit, Buddy!" Andi commanded. Buddy sat down. "See how good he is?" Andi said.

Mike reached the steps leading up to the front porch. "He knows I'm afraid of him," he fretted.

"Don't worry, dogs forgive anything." *Even being abandoned?* Andi wondered silently, picturing the Lab's adorable little face.

"So, what do you want me to do now?" Mike asked.

"Come and pet him."

Mike leaped back. "No way!"

"He won't hurt you, I promise."

Mike swallowed hard. He took a step toward Buddy, then stopped again. "He's got sharp teeth."

"Buddy has never bitten *anyone*. And he's not going to start now." Andi was sure she was on the right track. Once she got Mike to pet Buddy, he'd be well on his way to conquering his fear of dogs. "Go on, stroke his head."

Mike took another step forward, then reached toward him. Buddy sat still, his tail wagging.

Mike gently touched the top of Buddy's head with one finger. Buddy's tail wagged harder. "See?" Andi said. "He likes you."

Mike scratched Buddy's ears, but Andi could see from the strained expression on his face that he expected Buddy to bite him at any moment.

Suddenly, a cat appeared at the end of the driveway. Buddy sprang up with a loud bark, and Mike leaped back. He landed awkwardly on the bottom step and fell over backward.

Buddy jerked on his leash. It slipped through Andi's fingers, and he went tearing across the front lawn. The cat took off, scrambling over a fence with a rattle of claws. Buddy raced after it, barking furiously. "Buddy!" Andi yelled. "Come here!"

Buddy skidded to a halt, and then he slunk slowly back to the house with his tail between his legs and his leash trailing behind him.

"I'm really sorry, Mike," Andi said, helping him up. "Are you all right?"

"I guess so," he said, nodding. "Listen, it was good of you to try to help me. Maybe I'd get over my fear of

dogs if I knew some friendly ones, but I think Buddy's a little too lively for me."

Andi shrugged. "You're probably right. But it might be worth trying again."

"No, thanks. What I need is a small, *quiet* dog to start off with. Anyway, I'd better get going." He jogged away down the street.

Andi went indoors, thinking about what Mike had said. "I know an ideal small, quiet dog," she told Buddy. "The dog with no name! She'd be perfect." She hurriedly unclipped Buddy's leash. "Stay, Bud," she said, then she dashed back outside.

She caught up with Mike at the end of the street. "Hey, I know the perfect dog!" she called. "She's a little Labrador puppy. She's not very well right now, because she was hit by a car, but she's really friendly. You'll love her, Mike, I just know it!"

"I don't know. . . ."

"You should come and meet her," Andi pleaded.

He smiled. "Maybe. If she really *is* quiet."

"Definitely. Can you meet me at four o'clock outside the ASPCA?"

"I'll be there," Mike promised. "I can tell I won't get any peace until I say yes."

*   *   *

Right after breakfast, Andi grabbed her mom's digital camera. She planned to take a few shots of the Labrador puppy while she was at the ASPCA with Mike. Then the Pet Finders could start working on the posters.

As she put the camera into her backpack, her mom came out into the hall. "What are you doing, Andi?"

Andi explained about the photos.

Her mom shook her head. "I'm sorry, honey, but that camera's way too valuable to take to school. You could lose it."

"But, Mom!"

"No," Mrs. Talbot said firmly. "You're not taking it, Andi, and that's final."

"Could you meet me after school, then, and bring the camera with you? It's really important. I won't have time to come home and get it. I'm meeting Mike Morgan at the ASPCA right after school."

Her mom sighed. "I can't today. I've got meetings all afternoon, honey."

"Mom!" Andi groaned.

This was the Pet Finders' hardest case yet. No one seemed to have lost a dog, and now they couldn't even make posters!

Chapter Seven

Mike was waiting for the Pet Finders when they arrived at the ASPCA center after school. "Hey there! I bet you thought I wouldn't show up."

"Of course not," Andi said, but she was secretly relieved to see him. After the way Buddy had behaved that morning, she'd been afraid he might have turned Mike off of dogs for life.

Fisher was sitting in the reception area doing some paperwork when they went into the center. "Hey," he said. "Come to see the puppy?"

"This is Mike Morgan, our mailman," Andi explained. "He wants to meet her."

"How is she today?" Natalie asked.

"Much better," Fisher said. "How are you doing with tracking down her owner? Molly's been calling some other ASPCA centers to see if anyone's reported losing a Labrador, but we haven't heard of anyone yet."

"We're still working on it," Tristan said.

"We were going to take some photos of her today," Andi told him, "but I wasn't allowed to take my mom's camera to school, so we'll have to fit it in some other time."

They went through to see the dog with no name. She was lying in her bed, but she stood up as soon as she saw them. "She doesn't look so stiff today," Andi said, feeling pleased.

"And her cuts seem to be healing," Tristan added.

"What do you think, Mike?" Natalie asked. "Do you like the look of her?"

"She looks pretty safe, so far," Mike said. "It's a shame all dogs aren't as small and cute as this one."

"She won't be this small forever," Andi warned him.

"Now she tells me!" He heaved a melodramatic sigh.

They opened the cage, and the puppy trotted out with her tail wagging and her clean golden fur shining.

"She is so gorgeous!" Natalie exclaimed. She reached into the cage to pick up a ball and rolled it across the floor. The puppy trotted after it. She carried the ball back and dropped it at Natalie's feet. As she reached for it, Andi grabbed her arm.

"Let Mike play with her," she whispered.

"Huh? Oh, sure." Natalie looked puzzled, but she handed the ball to Mike. He rolled it away and the puppy trotted off to fetch it, wagging her tail harder than ever. When she brought it back, she pounced on one of Mike's shoelaces and tugged it. "Hey, she's really playful," he laughed, smiling down at her.

"Will you be all right if we go now, Mike?" Andi asked. "We've got to go search for a lost guinea pig."

Natalie and Tristan stared at her in surprise.

"Sure." Mike didn't even glance around; he was too wrapped up in ruffling the puppy's ears.

"See you later, then," Andi said. The Pet Finders said good-bye to Fisher and went out into the bright sunshine.

"What was that all about?" Tristan demanded as soon as they were outside. "You got us out of there too fast to not have something up your sleeve."

"It's part of my plan to cure Mike's fear of dogs," Andi explained. "I tried getting him to pet Buddy this morning, but Bud was all riled up about a cat."

"And you thought the puppy would be quieter," Natalie said. "Good idea. I hope it works."

"I've been thinking about Cocoa," Tristan said as they headed for Cooper's Hill.

"Careful, Tris," Natalie warned. "You don't want to strain yourself."

Tristan made his usual face at her. "If she *has* been stolen," he went on, "then I think a kid must have taken her, because guinea pigs aren't valuable. It's not like an adult would steal her to sell. So if a kid took her, we might find her in one of the yards near the Jupps' house. A kid wouldn't have a car to take her away in."

"That's true," Andi said. "We should look out for hutches while we're searching and try to see what's inside."

They passed a corner store. "Look!" Natalie exclaimed, stopping beside some notices that were stuck in the window. One of them had a picture of a golden Labrador puppy on it. FOR SALE, the poster read. GOLDEN LABRADOR PUPPIES. There was a phone number listed at the bottom of it.

Natalie pulled out her phone. "Let's give them a ring."

"Why?" Andi asked, puzzled.

"Maybe they sold the dog with no name." She punched in the number.

After a few moments, she grinned at Tristan and Andi and gave them a thumbs-up. "Hello?" she said into the phone. "Yes, I saw your postcard advertising puppies for sale. I don't want to buy one, but I'm trying to find the owner of a golden Labrador puppy who's about ten weeks old. She's had an accident and — "

She broke off and listened for a moment. "Oh, I see." She sounded disappointed. "Do you know any other Labrador breeders who might . . . ?" Again she stopped to listen. "Right. Okay, thanks." She snapped her phone shut. "No good. The breeder's puppies are only four weeks old, and her last litter was born six months ago."

"What about other breeders?" Andi prompted.

Natalie shook her head gloomily. "That woman just moved to Orchard Park from New Jersey, and she doesn't know anyone here yet."

Andi could see her own disappointment reflected in Tristan's and Natalie's faces. But they couldn't waste time moping around outside a convenience store. They had a guinea pig to find.

"Come on," Andi said. "Let's go look for Cocoa."

They were soon at the Jupps' house. When Tristan rang the bell, Mrs. Jupp opened the door. "Did you find her?" she said eagerly.

Shane came running, his face bright with hope. Andi felt really bad for him. "Not yet," she admitted. "We actually came to see if she's turned up, but I guess she hasn't."

Shane's face fell.

"We saw the posters," Mrs. Jupp said, trying to sound positive. "Great job! Has anyone called you yet?"

"No," Andi told her. This visit was proving really tough. "We're going to search around here. Where have you looked so far?"

"In our backyard, and Shane went down the alley behind the house. We put out a dish of sunflower seeds, in case she finds her way back into the yard and is hungry. They're Cocoa's favorite, but they haven't been touched."

"Okay," Andi said. "We'll start looking in the alley." They'd searched the middle part of the alley before, but not the area immediately behind the house or farther up the hill.

"Come through the house," Mrs. Jupp offered, opening the door wide.

The Pet Finders made their way through to the yard and past the dish of sunflower seeds and the hutch where Sugar sat all alone. Shane trailed after them. "I really, really miss Cocoa. You will find her, won't you?"

"We'll do our best," Natalie promised. "Hey, can we

take the dish of sunflower seeds with us? Maybe she'll hear it rattling and come running."

"Okay!" Shane ran to get it.

They headed uphill first, shaking the sunflower seeds and listening hard for a guinea pig's distinctive *whoop whoop* in reply. But there was nothing to hear except birds singing and a few distant cars. They searched in the long grass and checked around the roots of trees, looking for hollows where a guinea pig might try to keep herself safe.

"Don't forget to look for hutches, too," Tristan reminded them. "She might have been taken to someone else's yard."

Andi stood on tiptoe to look over a fence. "Nothing in here." She moved to the next yard and peered over the wall. "There's one in this yard. I can barely see the roof. Give me a boost so I can see inside."

Tristan and Natalie lifted her up.

"I can see a little patch of brown fur! Maybe it's her." Andi craned her neck, her heart thudding with excitement.

"Hurry up!" Natalie groaned. "You're heavy."

Andi leaned farther over the wall until she could see the creature in the hutch. "It's a rabbit. Forget it." She dropped down, nearly landing on Tristan's toe.

They set off again. "There's another hutch here!" Natalie called after a few minutes.

Tristan and Andi ran to see. This hutch stood at the end of a yard that was fenced in by a hedge so sparse they could easily see through it. "There's something in there," Natalie said. "I saw it move." She bent a branch aside and pushed through the hedge to look into the hutch. "It's brown," she said excitedly. Then she drew back, sighing. "I'm not sure what it is, but it's definitely not a guinea pig. It's got a long tail."

Andi and Tristan pulled branches aside so they could look, too. "It's a ferret," Tristan said, disappointed.

Andi glanced back along the alley. They'd gone quite a way from the Jupps' back gate. She wasn't sure that Cocoa could have come this far on her own. Guinea pigs had tiny legs and got tired easily. "Maybe we should go back and search in the opposite direction," she suggested. "That way — " She broke off as a distinctive squeak rang out.

Chapter Eight

The Pet Finders raced along the alley, following the tiny squeal. The stones beneath their feet slid away as they ran, but they couldn't slow down. If the squeaking stopped, they might not be able to find the yard where the noise was coming from.

Despite the uneven ground, Andi was soon quite a way ahead of Tristan and Natalie. The squeak was much louder now, and she could hear it clearly above the crunch of the stones under her feet. She stopped running and looked around. The sound was coming from behind a tall, wood-paneled fence. Andi ran to the fence and sprang into the air, but she couldn't see over it. There was no way she could climb the fence — the boards were perfectly smooth. "I can't see over," she said, as Natalie and Tristan came panting up.

"Let me get my breath back, then we'll try lifting you," Tristan puffed.

Natalie bent over, hands on knees, breathing hard. She didn't look as if she could hoist a blade of grass into the air at that point.

Andi looked around. There was a tall tree growing outside the neighboring yard. "It's okay. I can climb that tree," she said.

She swung herself onto the lowest branch. She still couldn't see over the fence, so she climbed to the next branch and then the next. At last, she could see right into the yard. A guinea pig's hutch was standing against the fence on one side. And to Andi's horror, a fat tabby cat was hunched in front of the hutch, gazing in through the wire. No wonder the guinea pig was making so much noise!

"Shoo!" Andi yelled.

Her shout startled the cat. It spun around, but then leaped onto the roof of the hutch, its claws scratching against the waterproof felt.

"What is it?" Tristan looked up at Andi, his freckled face anxious.

"There's a cat hanging around the hutch."

The cat stretched one paw over the edge of the roof, hooked its claws through the wire, and began to pull.

The frightened guinea pig raced up and down, squeaking at the top of its voice. Andi could see that it wasn't Cocoa; it had smooth ginger-and-white fur.

"Get away!" she shouted at the cat.

It looked up at her, then yanked at the wire again. To Andi's relief, the door stayed shut. But, all the same, she had to help the panic-stricken guinea pig. *Not just pet finders — pet rescuers, too*, she thought. She stretched up and caught hold of one of the branches near the top of the tree, then shook it as hard as she could, making the leaves swish and rustle.

The noise wasn't loud, but it was enough to frighten the cat. It leaped off the hutch onto the fence and scrambled to the top, its claws scratching madly. It teetered at the top for a moment, looking from Andi to the hutch and back again, then it vanished into the next yard.

Andi climbed down from the tree. "It's gone," she said with relief as she wiped her hands on her jeans.

"Was it Cocoa?" Natalie asked.

"No. But the hutch was the same as Cocoa's, and the cat couldn't get the door open." She paused. "I don't see how Cocoa could have gotten out by herself. If a cat couldn't open the door, there's no chance of a guinea pig doing it."

"She must have been stolen, then," Tristan said.

"Let's not tell Shane right away," Andi said, imagining his dismay. "Maybe the posters will do some good. Someone might see Cocoa in a neighbor's backyard and call us." At this point, Andi almost hoped the guinea pig *had* been stolen. At least then, Cocoa would be someplace safe. If she was out on her own, with a hungry cat on the prowl . . . Andi shuddered.

"We haven't finished searching yet," Natalie reminded them.

They went on down the alley, but there was no sign of Cocoa anywhere. There were no more hutches, either. At last they reached the part of the alley that they'd already searched. "She's not here," Tristan said glumly.

Andi glanced at her watch. "There's still time to get my camera and take a few photos of the puppy before the ASPCA closes for the night." It would be good to have something positive to do.

"Will it involve running?" Natalie asked. "I've had more than enough exercise for one day, thank you."

Andi laughed. "No. We have enough time to walk. Come on."

Buddy was sitting in the hall when the Pet Finders reached Andi's house. He sprang up at her, barking excitedly.

"What's up, Bud?" Andi said. She crouched down to pet him, and he leaped onto her lap and licked her cheek. Then he jumped down again and went racing around Tristan and Natalie.

Andi's mom came into the hall. "Thank goodness you're home, Andi," she said, raising her voice to make herself heard above Buddy's excited barks. "Buddy's had a crazy half hour. He's been racing up and down the stairs and barking every time a car goes by. Could you take him for a walk, please?" She disappeared into the kitchen again, clearly agitated by Buddy's behavior.

"Sure!" Andi called after her. "We're going to see the puppy. It'll be good for her to meet another dog!" She got her mom's camera, then went into the kitchen. "Can I take a corncob? Remember how much Buddy liked them when he was young? I thought maybe the puppy would like them, too."

"Help yourself. There's a pack in the fridge," her mom replied.

Andi took an ear of corn and went back into the hall. Tristan was holding Buddy in his arms and the little dog was licking his nose. "Pets are so great," he laughed. "But even *you* aren't as great as Lucy, Bud."

Andi clipped on Buddy's leash. "It must be the spring weather making him act like this," she said. "Maybe he remembers all the sunshine we used to have when we lived in Florida." She could hardly believe that she'd been living in Orchard Park for nine whole months. She lifted Buddy out of Tristan's arms and set him down on the floor.

"Phew! He almost washed my whole nose right off," Tristan joked.

The little Jack Russell dashed to the door and pressed his nose to the crack, impatient to be let out. "See you later, Mom!" Andi called as Buddy yanked her out the front door and down the driveway.

The dog with no name was chewing the edge of her basket when they got to the ASPCA.

"Hi, girl," Natalie said, opening the cage door.

The puppy ran out, her tail wagging and her soft, thick ears perked, then darted away down the room.

"Did you see that?" Tristan asked. "She actually *ran*. She must be feeling better. Fisher was right about that dislocated hip. You'd never know she had an injured leg a couple of days ago."

"And her cuts hardly show at all," Natalie added. "She'll look great in the pictures."

The puppy trotted back to them, her brown eyes

shining. She and Buddy touched noses, then the little Labrador darted away to fetch her ball. She retrieved it and dropped it by Buddy's front paws.

"She's really good at fetching," Tristan said.

"That's what Labradors do," Andi told him. "Their real name is Labrador retriever. Hunters often have them as pets."

Buddy looked up at Andi and barked. "Okay, boy!" she said. "You can play for a while, but don't wear the puppy out."

As soon as he was off his leash, Buddy grabbed the ball and went tearing around the room with it wedged in his mouth. The puppy scampered after him, yapping with excitement.

"We have *got* to think of a name for her," Natalie said. She clutched Andi's arm. "Hang on! I've got the perfect name for her! Amabel."

"Amabel?" Tristan hooted.

"It's my cousin's name. It means lovable."

"Figures," he said, rolling his eyes to the ceiling.

"The puppy *is* lovable. It really suits her."

"No way," Tristan said.

"You like it, don't you, Andi?" Natalie said hopefully.

Andi made a face. "Not really. I mean, it's okay for a

person, but it's weird. And it definitely doesn't sound like a dog's name."

The door of Fisher's office opened. "I should have known you three would be behind this mayhem," he joked. He watched as the dog with no name lay down right in front of Buddy, forcing him to jump over her, his stumpy legs at full stretch. "I think she was still feeling the aftereffects of the anesthetic when you called earlier, but it's obviously worn off now. Her bruises are nearly gone, too, and the cuts are healing nicely. Any luck with finding her owner?"

"Not yet, but we're going to take some pictures of her for the posters," Andi said, holding up her camera.

"Good luck! Let's hope you can keep her still long enough to take them. Oh, and by the way, Mike was terrific with her. Very gentle. I hope he can find time to come again." Fisher went back into his office again.

"Hey, look at Buddy," Natalie said.

He had gone into the cage and was lying in the puppy's basket, panting hard. The puppy was trying to make him play again, picking up the ball, and dropping it beside him over and over.

"No way!" Andi laughed. "I've never seen Buddy worn out from playing before!"

"He did run about twenty miles on the way here,"

Natalie reminded her. They'd cut across the park, and Buddy had raced in giant circles the moment he was let off his leash. "He must have run around the pond a hundred times."

"Well, I hope he's not too exhausted to walk home," Andi said. "I don't like the idea of carrying him all the way. He may be small, but he's pretty heavy."

"I'll play with you, girl," Tristan told the puppy. He threw the ball across the room, then sat down and waited for the pup to bring it back to him. She bounded after it, her ears flopping and her huge paws almost getting in her way. Snatching it up, she galloped back and dropped the ball beside Tristan. As he reached for it, the puppy darted behind him and snatched the red notebook out of his pocket.

"Hey, give that back!" Tristan scolded.

The puppy looked up at him with her head to one side, then scurried to the other end of the room with the notebook in her mouth. Tristan jumped up to run after her, but she dodged him and squeezed behind a chair.

"Come on, guys! Give me a hand here," Tristan begged.

Andi and Natalie were laughing too hard to reply.

The Lab lay down in the corner and began to chew the plastic binder cover. "Help me get it back!" Tristan begged. "It's got all our case notes in it."

Still laughing, Andi took the corn out of her backpack and held it out to the puppy, who quickly abandoned the notebook and took the cob, then lay down to gnaw it, her tail thumping against the ground.

"Take her picture!" Natalie urged. "Before she starts tearing around again."

Andi snapped a few shots while Tristan grabbed his binder. Not surprisingly, the cover was dotted with tiny teeth marks. "Typical!" he joked. "You try and help lost puppies and all they do is eat your stuff!"

When Andi was satisfied with the photos, she clipped Buddy's leash back on. "Let's go, boy. Time to get home."

The little Labrador trotted over, holding the corncob in her mouth. The two dogs sniffed each other briefly, then the puppy climbed into her basket, flopped down, and began to gnaw the corn again.

"Bye, girl," Andi said. She patted the pup's soft golden head before fastening the cage door. "She seems pretty happy here," she remarked as she straightened up.

"That's because she's so sweet-natured," Natalie

pointed out. "But we really have to step up the search for her owner. I can't think of a dog that deserves a good home more than she does!"

"Let's write 'The dog with no name' at the top of the posters," Natalie suggested later when they were sitting down in Andi's mom's study.

"Awesome!" Andi agreed. "People will be really intrigued." She typed it in, then pasted in her favorite photo of the ones she'd taken earlier. It showed the puppy looking straight into the lens, her soft ears perked up as though she were listening.

"What else do we need to write?"

"How about 'Do you know this puppy?'" said Tristan, crouching down to pet Buddy.

The little Jack Russell rolled over so Tristan could rub his tummy, then squirmed over again, sprang up, and licked Tristan's cheek. "Yuck! Get off, Bud. I'm clean enough, thanks."

"That's what you think," Natalie said. "But Buddy knows better."

"There!" Andi clicked on the print icon. "We're definitely getting faster at making posters." As the first one came spooling out of the printer, she picked it up. "We'll

put these up after dinner, okay?" She sighed. "Let's hope
they work. We haven't had much luck with the puppy *or*
with Cocoa so far."

"I know what you mean," Natalie agreed. "I really
hope we're not going to fail with these two cases."

They looked at one another gloomily until Buddy
sprang into the middle of the room and began to chase
his tail. Then they all laughed.

"Thanks, Bud. You know how to cheer people up,
don't you?" Tristan said.

Andi glanced at the poster again. "We can't keep calling her 'the dog with no name.'" She stared hard at the
photo, trying to come up with an idea. "Hey! How about
Beauty? She's so pretty, it fits her perfectly."

Tristan snorted. "Beauty? I don't think so."

"Why not? She is beautiful."

"It's not right for her," Natalie said. "She's too ener-
getic. A dog named Beauty should be poised as well as
pretty."

Tristan waved his binder under Andi's nose. "Dogs
named Beauty don't go around wrecking people's note-
books."

"Okay," Andi said, "but we've got to call her something."

"Dinner's ready!" Mrs. Talbot called up the stairs.

Tristan leaped up. "Fantastic, I'm starving!" He raced out of the study and down the stairs.

"Do you know who he reminds me of?" Natalie sighed.

"Who?" Andi asked.

"My dog," she replied. "Jet comes running, too, when I call him for his dinner."

Chapter Nine

After school the next day, the Pet Finders headed for the Banana Beach Café. It was the sunniest place in Orchard Park, with yellow walls and rainbow-colored umbrellas shading the tables outside. Today, with the sun shining so brightly, the café looked dazzling.

"Whoa, I should have brought my shades," Tristan said as they stood opposite the café, waiting to cross the road.

"The puppy posters look good," Natalie noted, pointing to one on a nearby lamppost. They'd put up nearly all of them the evening before. "I wonder if anyone called while we were at school."

"I'll check," Andi said. She took out her cell phone and called her mom.

"Sorry, honey. No messages," Mrs. Talbot answered.

Andi hung up and shook her head. "Nada."

Suddenly, her phone began to ring. Her heart jumped and she answered quickly. "Hello?"

"Hi," said a man's voice. "Is this Andi?"

"Yes."

"This is Tim Saunders, Tristan's dad. Sorry to bother you, but he hardly ever carries his cell phone, and I need to speak with him."

"Don't worry, he's right here, Mr. Saunders."

Tristan's eyebrows shot up as she passed the phone to him. "Hey, Dad. What's up?" There was a pause while he listened, then his face lit up. "Awesome! Thanks, Dad."

"Share the good news," Natalie prompted when he ended the call.

"I've been hoping this would work out all day," Tristan said, beaming at her and Andi. "But I didn't want to mention it before, just in case it didn't."

"What?" Natalie demanded. "Don't keep us hanging."

Tristan spread his hands wide like a magician. "The puppy's going to be in the local paper tomorrow! My dad knows an editor, and she sent a photographer to the ASPCA today to take the puppy's picture. They've written an article asking if anyone knows who she belongs to."

"You are amazing, Tris!" Andi said, giving him a hug.

But Natalie nudged her. "Watch it! Don't give him an excuse for an even bigger ego!" Then she laughed. "Seriously, it's great news, Tris. I bet someone will claim the puppy as soon as the paper comes out."

They crossed the road to the café and found Jango and Maggie Pearce — Fisher's parents, and owners of the café — sitting outside, studying a street map of Orchard Park.

"Hi, Maggie. Hi, Jango," Tristan called.

"Tristan! And Andi and Natalie!" Maggie jumped up. She was a round-faced Jamaican woman with a broad, welcoming smile. As always, she was wearing a bright sunshine-yellow dress. "How you doin'? You still searching for lost pets?"

"Yep," Andi said. She glanced at the map. "Are you trying to find something? Tristan can probably tell you how to get there. He knows just about every street in Orchard Park."

"Mansfield Road," Jango said. He was a middle-aged man with gray hair that grew in tufts on either side of his head. "There's a new flour mill there, and we heard their flour's the best anywhere. We only want the best for our banana muffins! But the writing on this map is so small, we can barely make it out."

"It's on the east end of town," Tristan told him. "Al-

most out in the country. Look." He bent over the map.
"Here."

"Tristan, you are a wonder, boy," Jango said, slapping
him on the back. "It's lucky you three are such regular
customers. We could have been searching for hours if
you hadn't stopped by. Now, what can we get you?"

"Banana-oat bars and apple juice, please," Tristan
said.

"You sitting outside in the sunshine?" Maggie asked.

"Yes, please," Natalie replied. "It's too nice to be indoors on a day like this."

"Be right out," Maggie said and disappeared inside
with Jango.

Andi was still looking at the map. "Isn't this where we
found the puppy?" She ran her finger along the main
road that headed south from Orchard Park.

"That's right," Tristan said.

"I wonder where her owners were going," Natalie said,
sounding puzzled. "That road looks as though it goes
straight out of town."

Andi's stomach turned over. She'd been trying not
to believe Tristan's theory that the puppy had been
dumped, but too many things seemed to point to it. For
a start, nobody had reported the dog missing. Nobody
had called since the posters went up, either, though the

town center was filled with them and it would be hard for anyone to miss them. Finally, and most important, the puppy had been found on a busy road that headed straight out of town.

"Maybe they *were* heading out of town," Andi said. "Maybe they were leaving Orchard Park for good." She shivered. "You might be right after all, Tris, about her being dumped."

Natalie started to argue, but Tristan interrupted. "Let's think about this logically. If Andi's right and her owners have moved out of town, then that would give them the perfect opportunity to dump her."

"Their old neighbors wouldn't know the puppy had disappeared," Andi figured angrily, "and their new ones wouldn't know they'd ever owned a dog."

Natalie shook her head. "I don't believe it. She's too lovable to just be thrown away."

Mike Morgan came jogging along the road then. He spotted the Pet Finders and came over to speak to them. "Hey, am I glad to see you!" He dropped into the empty chair at their table. "Marathon training can get a bit lonely."

"Do you run marathons at this time of year?" Tristan asked.

"Training for them is a year-round job." Mike's eyes

twinkled. "And you never know, I might find a publisher for my book, and I'll have to look good for the publicity photos." He had told Andi he was writing a book called *Mad Mike Morgan's Marathon Manual*. "Anyway," he continued, "I want to hear how the puppy's doing. I've seen posters of her all over town. Have you found her owner yet?"

"Not yet," Andi admitted. "We were wondering if they might have moved out of town. . . ." She trailed off and stared at Mike. "You're a mailman. You must know who's moved away recently."

"Sure, some of the families."

"Could you think of any names, so we can find out whether any of them used to have a golden Lab?"

Mike thought for a moment. "Hmmm."

Tristan handed Mike the red notebook. "You can write them in here."

Mike fingered the tooth-marked cover and grinned. "Looks like you three have been having a little dog trouble, too."

Maggie came out of the café carrying a tray of apple juice and oat bars while Mike was writing the list. There was a yellow paper umbrella and a rainbow-colored straw in every glass. "Hi there, Mike," she said. "Can I

get you something? A banana sandwich, maybe, to keep your strength up?"

"No, thanks, Mrs. P. I'll be off in a minute." He wrote down the last name. "Those are the only ones I can think of right off the bat. If I remember any others, I'll put the names in your mailbox with your mail tomorrow, Andi." He stood up. "I might see you when I go to visit the puppy."

"He seems to be getting along really well with the dog with no name," Andi mentioned as Mike jogged away.

They read through Mike's list of names as they sipped their apple juice. There were twelve altogether. "It'll take ages to check all these out," Natalie sighed. "I wonder if we can trim it down?"

Tristan stabbed his finger down on a name. "These people — the Wilkinsons — don't have a dog. James Wilkinson's a friend of Dean's, and I went to their apartment a few times." He crossed that name off, then sat staring into space.

"What are you thinking?" Andi asked.

"That we should find out which of these other people lived in apartments, too. People in apartments might be less likely to own dogs. Maybe they thought it would be nice to have a dog, but once they got one, they found they needed a yard and more space."

"So, what are we going to do?" Tristan broke off a piece of oat bar and put it in his mouth.

"Christine might recognize some of these names," Andi said. "She could eliminate people with cats, who might not have a dog, or true animal lovers who'd never dump a pet in a million years."

"I'll ask her tomorrow. I'm helping out at the store in the morning."

"Hang on. Shouldn't we tell Shane that we think Cocoa's been stolen?" Andi pointed out. Then she made a face. "Though I'm not looking forward to it much."

"We should all go together tomorrow," Tristan said. "I'll be finished by eleven. Can you wait until then?"

"Okay. Are you free then, Nat?"

"Yeah. Do you want to take Buddy and Jet for a walk before that? We could stop in to see the puppy, too."

"Great," Andi agreed.

Tristan ate the last morsel of his oat bar and drained his glass. He looked hopefully at Andi's oat bar. She'd been so busy thinking about the list of names that she hadn't eaten it yet. "I don't suppose you're done with that, are you?" he asked hopefully.

"No, she's not," Natalie answered on Andi's behalf. She wrapped the oat bar in a paper napkin. "She was planning to eat it on the way home," she said, and pushed it into Andi's pocket.

Andi laughed. "Sorry, Tris, but there's no way I'd miss out on Jango's home cooking. His oat bars are to die for."

Tristan sighed, then put the notebook into his backpack. "Then I'm not sure I'll be able to ask Christine about this tomorrow," he said in a faint voice.

"Why not?" Andi asked anxiously. "You just suggested it."

"Because I might die of hunger on my way home."

Natalie patted his arm. "Don't worry, Andi and I will come to your funeral." She linked arms with Andi and they set off down the road together.

"Hey, wait for me!" Tristan ran after them.

"Look at that," Natalie laughed. "A miraculous recovery! Now let's hope we get another miracle to help us solve these cases."

Chapter Ten

Andi and Buddy arrived at the ASPCA at ten o'clock next morning. It was another beautiful day, and Buddy was full of energy.

"Calm down, Bud," Andi said as they waited for Natalie and Jet.

Buddy jumped up and planted his front paws on her leg. His mouth was open in a wide grin.

Natalie and Jet appeared at the end of the road. Jet spotted Buddy and gave a friendly bark. Buddy began to pull toward him, his tail wagging eagerly.

"Hi," Natalie said. "Sorry I'm late. I couldn't decide what to wear."

"I'm not surprised. Nice top, by the way." Natalie was wearing a lilac T-shirt with a sequined star on one shoulder.

"Thanks," Natalie replied. "I got it for my birthday, but I've only worn it a couple of times. Are those cargo pants new?"

"Yep." Andi did a twirl to show them off.

Molly was feeding the baby bird again when they arrived at the clinic. "Hi," she said. "Come to see the puppy?"

"Yeah," Andi said. "And then we're taking Buddy and Jet for a walk in the park."

Molly suddenly looked hopeful. "I don't suppose you could take the puppy, too, could you? She's well enough for more exercise now, and Fisher's given her the shots she needs." The baby bird began to chirp loudly, and Molly dropped a morsel of meat into its beak with a pair of tweezers.

"Of course!" Andi exclaimed.

The puppy was very excited to be outdoors. Her paws seemed to go everywhere but in a straight line while she trotted beside Buddy and Jet. Her head turned constantly from side to side as she tried to look in every direction at once. She was the most inquisitive creature Andi had ever seen! A fly buzzed past, and the puppy snapped at it, then stopped to sniff a flower. The pollen made her sneeze, and she shook her head, her brown eyes wide with astonishment.

"You remember when we found Apple?" Natalie asked slowly.

"Yeah?"

Natalie frowned. "Look, I know it's a long shot, but she was excited about trucks because her owner was a truck driver. Maybe the dog with no name will get excited about a particular color or make of car, and that might help us find her owners."

"It's worth a try. Let's take her up to the highway where we found her."

The highway was packed with traffic when they arrived. As soon as they started walking along the sidewalk beside the ditch, the puppy began to tremble. She yapped bravely at a few racing cars, then tucked her tail between her legs and scuttled behind Andi, where she pressed herself against Andi's legs.

"I don't think this is going to work," Andi said. "She looks petrified." She picked the puppy up, trying to comfort her.

The little Labrador buried her face in Andi's shoulder. She was shaking all over. Buddy and Jet watched curiously with their heads to one side.

"Let's go," Andi muttered, swallowing a lump in her throat. "This isn't fair to her."

They hurried back, leaving the roaring traffic behind them.

When they were halfway down a quiet road, the puppy opened one eye and looked around.

"It's all right, girl, the cars are gone," Andi told her.

The puppy sat up in her arms and checked in every direction, then nudged Andi's chin with her head as if to tell her that she wanted to walk. Andi set her down, and she trotted back between Buddy and Jet, her tail wagging again.

"Poor little thing," Andi sighed. "It's no wonder she's terrified of traffic. She *was* hit by a car, after all."

"And maybe she associates cars with her owner," Natalie added grimly. "If she *was* dumped out of a vehicle, it's pretty likely that she'd be scared. It was a dumb idea. I should have realized how frightened she'd be."

Andi stared at her. "So you think she was dumped, too?"

Natalie nodded sadly. "I really hate the idea, but . . ." She shrugged. "Why hasn't anyone come forward to claim her? We've put up enough posters, and she's even been in the paper."

Andi watched as the puppy leaped up at Jet and nipped his ear. It made her heart ache to think that anyone could abandon such a creature.

They stayed on empty streets as they made their way to the Jupps' house. Tristan was sitting on a garden wall waiting for them when they arrived. He waved a piece of paper at them as they approached. "I've been through the list of names with Christine." He spread it out on the wall, then snatched it up hastily as the puppy tried to bite the corner. "No you don't, girl," he laughed, stroking her head.

"Did Christine recognize any of them?" Natalie asked.

"Four out of twelve. She seems to know just about every pet lover in Orchard Park — and where they all live. None of them had yellow Labs before they moved away."

"So, minus the Wilkinsons, we still have to investigate seven people," Natalie said. "That's going to take some time."

"Nope," Tristan said. "You're forgetting that my mom and dad work in real estate. They knew some of the names, too. Four more, to be exact."

"So, we've only got three names left on the list?"

"Yep."

"That's fantastic, Tris!" Andi exclaimed. "And — "

"Come on," Natalie interrupted. "We've got to break the news to Shane." She started up the driveway.

"I think we should get Shane's mom to call the police," Andi said quietly.

"But they're hardly likely to send out a squad car for a missing guinea pig," Natalie pointed out.

"Maybe other people have lost pets from their yards, too."

"Maybe." Natalie shrugged as she stepped onto the Jupps' porch. She seemed really down. "But we probably would have heard about them. We are the Pet Finders, don't forget."

Shane flung the front door open before they reached it. "Did you find her?" Mrs. Jupp appeared behind him, looking anxious.

"I'm afraid not," Andi confessed.

Shane's bottom lip began to tremble, and tears welled up in his eyes. "Let's go into your backyard," Andi said hurriedly. "So we can tell you what we think."

Mrs. Jupp took Shane's hand, and the Pet Finders followed them along the side of the house, exchanging worried glances. They'd never had to tell a pet owner that they were giving up a search before.

"The thing is, Shane," Andi began when they were in

the backyard, "we've looked all along the alley and in your neighbors' yards, and there's just no sign of Cocoa anywhere." She went to the hutch. "These bolts are very strong and we don't think Cocoa could have escaped by herself."

Shane stared at her wide-eyed, waiting for her to go on, but the words felt as though they were jammed in her throat.

"We think she must have been stolen," Natalie finished for her.

Mrs. Jupp gasped, and Shane burst into tears. His mom tried to hug him, but he pushed her away. "Will the police come?" he sobbed.

"Not for a — " Natalie began, but Tristan kicked her.

"It'd be kind of cool if they did," he said, and Andi guessed he was trying to cheer Shane up. After all, kids loved police cars, didn't they? "Especially if their car has the siren going and lights flashing!"

Shane cried harder than ever.

"Come here, honey," Mrs. Jupp said. She moved toward him but he darted away again.

"Nice one, Tris," Natalie hissed.

"I d-don't want the police to come!" Shane wailed.

"Why not?" Andi asked. "Maybe they'll find Cocoa and bring her home."

"Because I t-told a lie, and I'll g-get in trouble."

The Pet Finders stared at him.

"What lie?" asked Mrs. Jupp, perplexed.

"C-Cocoa wasn't in her hutch. I left her out in the yard by accident when . . . when you told me to clean my room. I f-forgot she was out and . . . and then we w-went sh-shopping. . . ."

"And when you got back, Cocoa was gone?" Tristan concluded.

Shane nodded. "I th-thought Mom would be m-mad at me if I said what really happened."

"Oh, Shane," Mrs. Jupp said. "Don't be silly! You can always tell me the truth." She picked him up, and the little boy wrapped his arms around her neck and clung to her, sobbing.

"What about the gate?" Andi asked. "Was it open, like you said?"

He shook his head.

The Pet Finders looked at one another. This changed things. Maybe they needed to look a little closer to home. They had focused their search farther away because there didn't seem to be any way Cocoa could have gotten out of the hutch or the yard on her own.

"Could we leave our dogs in your house while we look around a little more, Mrs. Jupp?" asked Andi.

"Sure, you can put them in the kitchen," Mrs. Jupp offered. "They'll be fine in there."

The Jupps' yard was basically a strip of grass surrounded by a concrete path that was edged with bushes. A shed stood near the back of the yard.

"Let's try the shed first," Andi said. "Guinea pigs tend to get hot, so Cocoa might have gone in there for some shade." She opened the door. The shed was very tidy, with garden tools hung neatly on hooks. The floor was clear, and they could see at once that Cocoa wasn't there.

"Let's search the bushes," Natalie suggested. She ran to the end of the yard nearest the house, Tristan headed for the gate, and Andi started searching in the middle. They crawled along on their hands and knees, lifting branches to peer underneath and calling Cocoa's name. But there was just no sign of her.

"Hey!" Tristan called suddenly. "There's a guinea pig–size hole in the fence between here and next door."

Andi ran to see. Tristan stood up, his eyes full of excitement. "And there's brown fur caught on the fence. She must have gone through!" He held out his hand to show a few strands of wiry, dark brown hair.

Shane raced up. "That's her hair!"

Andi stood on tiptoe to look over the fence, then groaned. The grass on the other side was knee-high, and the borders were packed with tall flowers and weeds, with shrubs so bushy that a whole family of guinea pigs could be hiding inside them. "This is going to take a while," she sighed. But at least there was a chance that Cocoa might have been able to hide from cats and raccoons in the miniature jungle.

"We'll have to go and ask your neighbor for permission to search his yard," Natalie said to Mrs. Jupp.

"No need," Mrs. Jupp told her. "He moved away a couple of months ago and the new people haven't moved in yet. Their back gate is unlocked. Shane has had to go in there a few times to find his baseball."

"Here goes, then," Natalie sighed as they went next door. "I hope I don't stain my jeans."

They started by searching a flower bed close to the hole in the fence. The flowers were tangled with thistles and weeds. "This would be a good place for her to hide," Tristan said. "Guinea pigs are pretty nervous, so this tangle would make her feel safe."

"How come you're suddenly an expert on guinea pigs?" Natalie asked.

"I read up on them at Paws for Thought this morning, while I was waiting for a delivery to arrive."

Andi spotted a dandelion with frilly leaves, looking as if it had been nibbled to death by sharp little teeth. She yanked it out of the ground. "Do guinea pigs eat dandelion leaves, Tris?"

"Love 'em," Tristan replied.

"She could have come this way, then. Let's see if we can find any more."

There was another half-eaten dandelion growing under a rosebush, and a row of overgrown lettucelike plants had tiny teeth marks all over them.

"Guinea pigs spend about six hours a day eating," Tristan told them. "Lucky for us, it means she's left us a trail to follow."

They kept searching. Natalie soon found that the base of a picnic table had been gnawed. "She definitely came this way," she said. "Her teeth marks are really clear in this wood. Where was she heading?"

At last, Andi spotted a patch of wet mud where Cocoa's tiny paw prints were clearly visible. "This is it, guys. She was definitely here," she said. "Her claws have made pretty deep holes in the soil."

"I wonder if she's gone into that shed," Natalie said. "If she likes safe places, she might have snuck in there. I'll see if the door's open."

At the same time, Andi bent back a bramble and crawled through a narrow gap between a rosebush and a clump of thorny shrubs, peering around in all directions for more evidence that the guinea pig had been that way.

Suddenly, she heard Natalie's voice again. "Come and see this!"

Andi stood up. Natalie was standing in the shed doorway. She was covered from head to toe in cobwebs, and there was a dirty smudge on her nose, but she was wearing a huge grin.

Andi and Tristan raced over to her. "Did you find Cocoa?"

Natalie stood aside so that they could see past her into the shed. For a moment, after the sunny brightness of the yard, Andi couldn't make out anything. Then her eyes became accustomed to the gloom, and she saw that the shed was almost empty. A workbench stood under a grimy window, covered with dust and webs. Beneath it was a pile of burlap sacks, and in the middle of the heap crouched Cocoa.

But not just Cocoa! Beside her were four tiny baby guinea pigs, two brown, one white, and one black.

"No way!" Andi breathed. She crouched down beside the guinea-pig nest and stroked Cocoa with one finger.

"It's okay, girl. We're going to take you and your babies home!"

"I didn't realize guinea pigs were born with their fur," Natalie whispered. "I thought they'd be hairless, like rats and mice." She bent down to pet the babies and they squirmed toward her, giving tiny squeaks.

"Do you think Cocoa will bite me if I pick her up?" Andi asked. She touched the guinea pig cautiously, but Cocoa didn't seem bothered, so she lifted her up. The guinea pig settled down in her hands so trustingly that Andi realized Shane must be a good guinea-pig owner — even if he was a little forgetful!

Natalie and Tristan each picked up two of the babies. Then they went out of the shed into the sunshine.

"I'm very impressed, Nat," Tristan said. "I never would have thought you'd go inside that filthy shed."

Natalie shrugged. "Someone had to do it. And I'm glad I did, since we've solved another case. Let's hope the dry cleaners do as good a job with my outfit." Tristan and Andi laughed, and Cocoa squeaked in alarm.

"Sorry, little one," Andi apologized.

As they went back into the Jupps' yard, Shane and his mom came running over quickly. "Did you find her?" Shane cried. "I thought I heard her squeaking!"

"She's right here." Andi placed the guinea pig in his

hands. Cocoa snuggled against him, giving tiny whooping murmurs, a bit like purring.

"She wasn't the only guinea pig we found," Natalie said. She and Tristan bent down so Shane could see the four babies.

"Babies!" he said with delight. He turned to look at his mom, his eyes shining. "Mom, Cocoa had babies!"

Mrs. Jupp smiled weakly. "What a surprise! I never would have guessed Cocoa was expecting. And we always thought Sugar was a girl." She sighed. "I guess that means we'll need another hutch to keep the two of them apart."

"I sometimes help out at Paws for Thought, the pet store on Main Street," Tristan said. "I'm sure Christine Wilson, the owner, would be happy to swap Sugar for a girl guinea pig. And she'd take the babies, too, when they're old enough to leave their mother."

Mrs. Jupp smiled. "It looks like you've covered all the bases. But I'll have to talk to Shane about swapping Sugar. I'll put her — I mean *him* — in the glass tank indoors for now, where the guinea pigs live during the winter, so Cocoa and her babies won't have to share." She lifted Sugar out of the hutch gently. "Come on, girl — oops, boy," she corrected hastily. "You're coming inside with me." She headed toward the house, then stopped by the French doors and turned back to the Pet Finders. "Thank you so much for all your help. You've done a great job."

"We enjoyed it," Andi said. "And we're glad everything turned out okay."

She opened the sleeping compartment of the hutch, and Shane placed Cocoa inside. She turned in a little circle, flattening a nest in the hay. Tristan and Natalie put the babies in it, and Cocoa began to rearrange the hay around them to keep them warm.

"We'd better go," Natalie said as Andi shut the hutch door again. She gazed down at her filthy clothes. "I *so* need a bath."

"Thanks for finding Cocoa!" Shane said, his eyes shining. "And the babies are awesome! I promise I'll never, ever leave them outside the hutch."

"Glad we could help," Tristan said.

They got the dogs from inside, then set off for the ASPCA to take the puppy back.

Chapter Eleven

"This feels so great!" Tristan exclaimed. "We thought Cocoa was gone for good, and in the end we found Shane four extra guinea pigs!"

"It's perfect!" Natalie agreed. "We've done it again!"

"But this time was different," Andi pointed out. "We'll have to watch out for owners not telling the truth in the future. Where's that list of names, Tris?" she added. "Maybe our good luck with Cocoa will spill over into the puppy's case."

He fished out the list, and they all gathered around to look at it.

"Hey, I recognize this name," Andi said. "Griffith. My friend Chen's always going on about his friend Ashleigh Griffith. She lives right next door to him. I wonder if it's her family who's moved, or some other Griffiths."

"Do you know where Chen lives?" Natalie asked.

"Oriole Way. I took a get-well card to him last week because he's had an ear infection."

"Would he know whether his neighbors had a dog or not?" Tristan asked.

"Of course," said Andi. "They were best friends."

"Let's head over. It's only a couple of blocks away, right?"

Andi nodded. "What are we waiting for?"

"I can't go anywhere like this," Natalie wailed. "My reputation will be shattered if I show up at Chen's house covered in cobwebs."

"We'll clean you up," Andi said. She picked a sticky cobweb off Natalie's shoulder. "You don't have time to go home and change."

It didn't take long to brush the worst of the dust off of Natalie's clothes. Andi wiped away a smudge from her friend's nose, and they set off on the two-block walk to Chen's house.

"I'll wait outside with the dogs," Natalie offered. "Maybe our dog with no name will recognize her old home and give us a clue." She was obviously convinced she still wasn't presentable.

Chen's mother, Mrs. Lu, showed them up to his bedroom. She seemed pleased that he had some visitors.

Chen was lying on his bed in pajamas, watching television. Model airplanes hung from the ceiling, and there were dozens of others half-built on his desk and chest of drawers.

His face brightened when they went in. "Am I glad to see you guys!" he said, switching off the television and sitting up. "I'm bored to death in here, but my mom thinks I'll get sick again if I don't rest."

"You could finish making one of these planes," Tristan suggested, picking up a wing.

Chen shrugged. "I've had enough of planes for a while. Sticking little pieces of plastic together is pretty much all I've been doing for the last week."

"Are you feeling better?" Andi asked.

"Tons. With any luck, I'll be back in school on Monday."

Tristan gaped at him. "Are you kidding? You're actually looking forward to getting back to school?"

"Yes! It's no fun being home now, anyway. My friend Ashleigh from next door moved out of town."

Andi and Tristan looked at each other excitedly. "I don't suppose she had a dog, did she?" Andi asked.

"Yeah. Her uncle bought her a puppy for her birthday. How did you know?"

"We found a lost puppy, and we think it might belong to someone who's moved away," Tristan explained.

"What breed was Ashleigh's puppy?" Andi asked.

"I don't know. I only caught a glimpse of it a couple times. They just had it about a week. Before we knew I had an ear infection, my mom thought my allergies were causing my headaches, so I wasn't allowed to go see the dog. I know it was yellow, though."

A mixture of hope and anxiety stirred inside Andi, and from the expression on Tristan's face, she could tell that he was feeling the same.

"When did Ashleigh move, Chen?" Tristan said.

"At the end of last week. Thursday, I think."

"We've got to get inside the house next door," Andi whispered.

"Good thinking," Tristan agreed. "We have to go, Chen," he added abruptly.

Chen's face fell. "But you just got here."

"Sorry," Andi said. "This can't wait. We'll come back and see you later."

She and Tristan raced out of the room, downstairs, and out the front door.

Natalie was sitting in the yard. Buddy and Jet were lying beside her, and the puppy was curled up in her arms, fast asleep.

"I tried to watch to see if the puppy recognized the house, but I couldn't tell," she explained. "She looked excited for a minute, but then she just settled down to take a nap. I wonder if it's because she's sad."

Andi and Tristan quickly explained what they'd learned from Chen.

"Wow! Good work!" she exclaimed. "We are getting really good at this, guys."

"Not so fast. We still need to find out what type of puppy Ashleigh had," Andi said. "Lots of breeds have yellow fur. Come on!" She sprinted around to Chen's neighbor's house.

"What are we going to say?" Tristan asked as Natalie rang the bell. "The new people might not know anything about Ashleigh's puppy."

"We've got to prove that she used to live here," Natalie said. "Then we can track them down."

There was no time to say anything else, because the door was opened by a red-haired woman in her early thirties. "Hello," she said, smiling at them.

"I — um — That is, we . . ." Tristan looked around helplessly at the other Pet Finders.

Andi tried to think of something to say, but her mind was blank. What kind of evidence might prove that the puppy had once lived here?

"Can we look for pet hair in your house, please?" Natalie said.

The woman's mouth dropped open. "Pet hair?" she echoed. "What on earth are you talking about?"

"We think a Labrador puppy used to live here," Andi added, afraid that the woman might close the door. "We're the Pet Finders Club, and we're trying to find her owners. She's lost."

"I see. Well, you might be at the right address. My husband and I didn't see a dog when we looked at the house, but one must have moved in here after we'd agreed to buy it. I'm allergic to dog hair, and I sneezed nonstop for the first two days after we moved in."

"Could we come in, then, please?" Andi asked. She crossed her fingers for luck. It would be terrible if the woman turned them away when they were so close to finding out the truth.

"I guess you can, although I'm not sure you'll find anything. My husband went through the house with the vacuum cleaner pretty thoroughly. And you'll have to leave those dogs outside, I'm afraid."

"I'll hold them," Tristan offered. He took Jet's and Buddy's leashes and Natalie carefully transferred the sleeping pup into his arms. The puppy opened one eye and yawned widely, then settled down again with a contented sigh.

"I'm Mrs. O'Donnell," the woman added.

"I'm Andi, and this is Natalie," Andi said as they stepped inside. She glanced around eagerly but, to her dismay, the house was spotless. "This place is even cleaner than your house, Nat," she whispered.

They followed Mrs. O'Donnell from room to room. The living room and kitchen had polished wooden floors, and Andi and Natalie exchanged an anxious glance. "I don't think we'll find much fur here," Nat said in a low voice. "Hardwood floors are really easy to clean."

Upstairs, the bedrooms were carpeted and Andi's hopes soared. Surely there'd be a few hairs remaining here. She got down on her hands and knees in a corner of the second-biggest bedroom, guessing that this might have been Ashleigh's room, but there wasn't a trace of hair to be found. They searched the other bedrooms, too, their anxiety growing by the second as they crawled backward and forward across the beige carpets.

"I didn't know my husband was so good at vacuuming," Mrs. O'Donnell laughed. "I'll have to start renting him out."

"I guess that's that," Natalie said miserably when they were standing in the hall again. "We've run out of leads."

"Hang on," Andi gasped. "What about the vacuum

cleaner? I bet that will turn up some evidence!" She turned to Mrs. O'Donnell. "Do you think we could look at your vacuum cleaner?"

"Well, if you really want to." She got it out from the closet under the stairs. "But please take it outside if you're planning to empty it. The garbage can is around the side of the house."

Andi and Natalie hurried outside with the vacuum cleaner. "Any luck?" Tristan called.

"Not yet. But there might be some hair in here." Natalie disconnected the vacuum cleaner bag and tipped the dirt onto a sheet of newspaper beside the garbage can.

"Bingo!" Andi cried. Mixed in with the dust and fluff were hundreds of strands of yellow dog hair. Grinning broadly, she pulled out a small bunch of hair and ran over to hold it against the puppy's coat. It was the wrong color.

"Oh, no!" Andi groaned. "She didn't belong to Ashleigh!"

"No, wait," Tristan said. "Her fur's paler underneath. Look." He tilted the puppy slightly and they saw that she was much lighter on her tummy. The pale hairs were a perfect match.

Natalie searched the vacuum cleaner again. "These

look darker," she said, pulling out a few strands of hair the color of dark honey. She held them against the fur on the puppy's back. "The color's identical here, too. She *must* have lived in this house! Now we've got to find out whether she's lost or abandoned."

"We'll have to call her old owners," Tristan said. "Let's ask Chen if he's got Ashleigh's new phone number."

"I'll go." Andi darted back to Chen's house and rang the bell.

By the time she came back, Tristan and Natalie had put the vacuum cleaner back together and returned it to Mrs. O'Donnell.

"You could call her on your cell phone right now, Nat," Tristan said.

Natalie shook her head. "I don't think this is the sort of call *we* should make. Maybe we should ask Fisher to do it. I mean, this is pretty serious stuff — especially if they deliberately dumped the puppy on the highway."

Tristan started to argue, but Andi interrupted. "Natalie's right. It would be best if Fisher called Ashleigh's mom."

"Let's go ask him to do it," Natalie said. Her voice shook, and Andi squeezed her arm. She knew exactly how Natalie felt. They'd almost found the puppy's owner, but this was very different from solving their other cases. Finding *this* owner might not be a cause for celebration.

"Wow! This puppy weighs tons more than Lucy," Tristan complained as the Pet Finders reached the ASPCA. "I'll be glad to put her down."

Fisher was in his office when they went inside. "Hi," he said. "Good walk?"

"We think we found out who owns the puppy!" Andi burst out. "It's a girl named Ashleigh Griffith."

"She moved to Pemberton," Tristan added. Pemberton was a town about an hour's drive from Orchard Park.

Fisher put down his pen. "Have you spoken with her?"

"Not yet. It felt . . . sort of . . . wrong for us to call."

Fisher understood what Andi meant. "You mean, in case her family abandoned the puppy?"

They nodded, almost ashamed to agree.

"Okay," said Fisher. "Give me the phone number and I'll speak to Ashleigh's mom or dad."

Andi read it to him, and he jotted it down on a message pad. "Right. You three go put the puppy back in her cage, and I'll come to find you when I'm finished."

The puppy had a drink of water, then flopped contentedly into her basket and fell asleep. Buddy lay down beside the open cage door while Jet licked her empty food bowl and looked hopefully up at Natalie.

"What do you think Fisher's saying?" Andi wondered, glancing at the door. "I really hope the puppy was only lost and that Ashleigh wants her back. She wouldn't have seen the posters or the newspaper in Pemberton." But there was a nagging doubt at the back of her mind. If Ashleigh loved the puppy so much, why hadn't she reported her missing?

"This case is the most difficult we've ever had," Tristan sighed. "Trying to find an owner who might not want to be found — " He broke off as Fisher appeared in the doorway. "What did they say?"

He sighed. "It's a no-go, guys. I'm really sorry. I spoke to Mrs. Griffith. She says they don't have a dog — never have."

"But that's not true!" Natalie exclaimed. "We saw the puppy's fur in Mrs. O'Donnell's vacuum cleaner."

"I know it looks suspicious," Fisher agreed, "but all golden Labs have hair about this color. Maybe another golden Lab visited the Griffiths before they moved." He shrugged. "It was a great lead, guys, but to be honest, I don't see what else I can do. I have to take Mrs. Griffith's word that they've never had a dog." The phone started to ring then, and he went to answer it.

"That means we still don't know for sure who the puppy's owner is," Andi said miserably. "This is hopeless! We can't find a new home for her until we know that her old owner definitely doesn't want her back."

"I guess we just got it wrong, and we'll have to keep searching," Tristan said.

"But we know Ashleigh had a puppy because Chen said so," Andi pointed out. "Mrs. Griffith *must* be lying!"

"That's right!" Natalie said fiercely. "We'll just have to make the Griffiths admit that the puppy belonged to them!"

Andi frowned. "But how?"

There had to be a way. If only they could figure out what it was.

Chapter Twelve

"Lunch," Tristan said. "That's what we need."

"How can you think about food at a time like this?" Natalie challenged him. "We've just reached a dead end in our search for the puppy's owner, and all you're worried about is eating."

"We need to think," Tristan pointed out. "And it's already two o'clock. I always think better on a full stomach."

"We might as well go," Andi said. "Hanging around here's not going to change anything."

They said a quick good-bye to the puppy and headed outside. "There's a deli on the corner," Tristan said. "Let's get some sandwiches and eat them in the park. Then we can talk about what to do next."

They found an empty bench near the pond. Andi didn't feel much like eating, so she shared her bagel with Buddy. She was angry and frustrated. What they needed was to speak to Ashleigh — maybe then they'd find out the truth about the puppy. But if they called Ashleigh, she might tell the same story that her mom did. Who knew what was going on?

Suddenly, she had a brainstorm. "I know!"

Tristan and Natalie turned to her eagerly. "What?"

"I'll call Ashleigh and offer her the dog-training DVD I used when Buddy was a puppy. I'll tell her I know Chen so she won't be suspicious."

"Here, use my cell phone." Natalie handed it to her, and Andi punched in the number. She held her breath, willing Ashleigh to pick it up.

"Hello?" said a girl's voice after a few rings.

"Is Ashleigh home?" Andi asked.

"This is Ashleigh."

"Hi, my name's Andi. I'm a friend of Chen's. He told me you've got a new puppy, and I wondered if you'd like my dog-training DVD. It worked wonders with my Jack Russell terrier, Buddy." She glanced around for Buddy and saw him chasing ducks at the edge of the pond. The ducks were waddling away as fast as they could. "Of course, I know your dog isn't a terrier . . ." Andi paused, hoping Ashleigh would say something.

"No, she was a golden Lab. But I don't have her anymore. My uncle bought her for me without checking if we actually wanted a dog first. I tried really hard to look after her, but it was impossible to fit everything in. I play the flute, and I'm also a gymnast. And then there's homework. Luckily, my mom managed to find a new home for the puppy."

"Oh." Andi gave Tristan and Natalie a cautious thumbs-up. "When? Chen didn't tell me that."

"We moved last week, and I went to stay with my grandparents for a couple of days while my mom and dad organized everything. When I came back, the puppy was gone."

"You must have been so upset when you found out," Andi said, imagining how she'd feel if her mom gave Buddy away.

"I was sad at first," Ashleigh agreed. "But I know it's for the best. Puppies need a lot of attention, and I just couldn't give her as much time as I wanted."

"I guess you don't need the DVD, then."

"I guess not. Thanks for asking, though. Bye."

Andi hung up, pressing the OFF button much harder than she needed to. She wasn't angry with Ashleigh, but the way Mrs. Griffith had lied made Andi's blood boil.

"What did she say?" Tristan asked.

"Is the puppy hers?" Natalie demanded.

"Yes, but Ashleigh didn't have enough time to look after her," Andi blurted out. "Mrs. Griffith told Ashleigh that she'd found a new home for the puppy, so her mom must have been the one who dumped her."

"You didn't tell her that the puppy's turned up?" Natalie said.

"No way!" She simply would not tell Ashleigh that the puppy had been found, in case the Griffiths decided they wanted her back after all. That puppy deserved a home where people had time for her!

Buddy trotted over, and Andi picked him up and hugged him. He licked her chin.

"Let's go back to the clinic and tell Fisher what we've found out," Tristan said. "Did Ashleigh tell you the puppy's name, Andi?"

Andi stared at him in dismay. "Uh-oh! I forgot to ask!"

The Pet Finders took Buddy and Jet home before heading back to the ASPCA. Andi needed a walk to calm herself down — talking to Ashleigh had upset her more than she wanted to admit.

Fisher was on the phone when they arrived. They waited outside his office door until he hung up. "This phone hasn't stopped ringing since you left," he said. "Just about all of Orchard Park saw the puppy in the paper and wants to offer her a home." He laughed. "It looks like you'll have to hold interviews if you don't manage to find her real owner first."

"Oh, we found her real owner, all right," Tristan said grimly.

The Pet Finders told Fisher about Andi's phone call to Ashleigh. He sighed and shook his head. "If only people would make sure pets are wanted before they give them as presents! Still, we can treat the puppy as a stray now and find her a new home." His attention was diverted out the window then. "Who's this?"

Through the window, they saw that a red car had pulled up outside. A tall woman in a blue dress climbed out. She hurried toward the door of the building.

"I'm Mrs. Griffith," she said anxiously as she breezed into the reception area and approached the desk. "I've come to see Dr. Pearce."

"It's Ashleigh's mom!" Natalie hissed.

Andi's knees felt as if they were going to buckle. There could only be one reason why Mrs. Griffith had turned up at the ASPCA — she'd guessed that the puppy had been found and now she'd changed her mind and wanted her back.

"Quick!" Andi said. "In here!"

The Pet Finders darted into the animal unit. The

puppy was still asleep. "We've got to get her out of here," Andi decided. "There's no way she's going home with that woman!"

They opened the cage door. "Come on, girl!" Natalie picked her up.

"Hang on," Tristan warned. "We're Pet *Finders*, not pet*nappers*."

"You don't want her to go back to someone who dumped her on the highway, do you?" Andi demanded.

Tristan shook his head, took the puppy from Natalie, and tucked her inside his jacket. She popped her head out and licked his chin.

Natalie pushed her down again. "You've got to stay in there," she warned. "It won't be for long, I promise."

"Come on," Andi said. They hurried to the door, and Andi opened it. To her dismay, Mrs. Griffith was talking to Fisher in the hallway that led to the reception area. They'd have to walk right past her.

"I wasn't entirely truthful with you on the phone earlier, Dr. Pearce," Mrs. Griffith said. "We did have a puppy, but I lost her. And when you called, I couldn't say anything because my daughter was there. You see, I told her I'd found a new home for her puppy but — " She spotted the Pet Finders and stopped.

"Hello," Andi said, forcing herself to smile. She knew

there was no way Mrs. Griffith would know her, but she couldn't help feeling scared. She walked along the corridor, trying to look casual, and squeezed past Mrs. Griffith. Tristan started to follow, but the puppy gave a tiny yap from inside his jacket.

The Pet Finders froze. Fisher's eyebrows shot up so high they almost vanished into his hair.

"We're . . . um . . ." Tristan began, trailing off as the puppy's head appeared just below his chin.

"Taking her out for some exercise," Natalie finished for him.

"She looked as though she needed some fresh air," Andi added hurriedly.

Mrs. Griffith gasped when she spotted the puppy. "Oh! You've found her! I'm so relieved." She ruffled the puppy's silky ears. "I've been so worried about her."

"Come into my office," Fisher said.

Mrs. Griffith went with him inside and sat down in a chair by his desk. The Pet Finders followed and perched on the windowsill. The puppy gazed around with her soft ears perked up.

"What actually happened?" Fisher asked.

"I was bringing the puppy here last Thursday, the day we moved to Pemberton. I know you can find homes for unwanted pets. I stopped for gas, but I must not have closed my car door properly. The puppy escaped. I realized she was missing as soon as I went back to my car."

Andi's anger toward Mrs. Griffith began to subside a little. Maybe she wasn't quite as bad as she'd thought.

"I searched forever," Mrs. Griffith continued, "up and down all the streets around the gas station, but there was no sign of her. And I kept thinking of all the things I still had to do — last-minute packing, organizing the moving men, getting the house ready for the new people who were moving in." She sighed. "And picking my daughter up from her grandparents' house. In the end, I had to give up the search and go home."

"I see," Fisher said. "Why didn't you report her missing?"

Mrs. Griffith swallowed hard. "I thought about it, but everything has been such a rush. I've hardly had a moment to myself. And Ashleigh, my daughter, has been home, helping me get organized. She starts at her new school on Monday. I told her I'd found a home for the puppy so she wouldn't be upset. I didn't want her to overhear me calling the ASPCA to tell them the puppy was lost."

"So you don't want the puppy back?" Andi checked. Although she knew now that Mrs. Griffith wasn't as bad as she'd feared, she was certain they weren't the right owners for the little Lab.

"Oh, no," Mrs. Griffith said hurriedly. "We never wanted a dog in the first place. My brother just turned up with her on Ashleigh's birthday. But my husband had gotten a job as a restaurant manager in Pemberton, and we were in the middle of moving there. We promised the new homeowners we'd be out by the first, and before I knew it, it was the thirtieth! They'd already stayed in a hotel for a few days while we finished up, so we had to leave quickly. And the temporary apartment they have us in above the restaurant — well, we simply can't have a dog there."

"So you'll be happy to let us re-home her for you?" Fisher asked.

"Oh, yes, please. It would be such a weight off my mind."

Fisher took a form out of his desk drawer and set it in front of Mrs. Griffith. "You'll need to fill this out."

"Of course. And can I give you a check to cover the cost of any treatment you've given the puppy?"

"A donation to the center would be welcome," Fisher said, smiling.

Mrs. Griffith filled in the form, then she wrote out a check and handed it to him.

"Thank you." Fisher tucked the check into the pocket of his white coat. "And don't worry about the puppy. She appeared in the local paper this week, and we've been swamped with calls from people who want to give her a home."

"I'm so pleased," Mrs. Griffith said. She stood up and stroked the puppy's head. "She's a dear little thing, and I'm really glad I came now. I had to come back to Orchard Park, anyway, to get the last of our things. I'd left them in a friend's garage." She headed for the door.

As she went out, Mike Morgan came in. "How's the world's sweetest puppy today?" he asked, smiling around at them.

"She's great," Andi told him. "And we've tracked down her owner!"

Mike's smile froze on his lips. "Oh." He sounded disappointed. "I've kind of gotten used to visiting her. I guess I'll miss her when she's gone."

"Don't worry, the previous owner doesn't want her back," Natalie told him.

"So, I'll be able to see her a while longer?"

"Yep," Fisher agreed.

"Do you know what?" Tristan groaned. "We didn't ask Mrs. Griffith the puppy's name."

"Well, whatever she's called, I've brought her some corncobs," Mike said. He spotted the pup peeping out of Tristan's jacket. "Hey, girl." He reached in to pet her. "How are you?"

The dog with no name scrambled her way out of Tristan's jacket and launched herself at him. Mike caught her, laughing, and held her close to his chest. "I guess you'll be looking for a new home for her now," he said.

Suddenly, Andi knew the perfect person to adopt the puppy. "You should adopt her, Mike!" she said. "You two are perfect together!"

"Me!" Mike's face lit up. Then his smile faded. "But I've never had a pet. I don't know the first thing about looking after a dog."

"You can learn, no problem. There are hundreds of books about caring for dogs," Fisher said, and handed him a leaflet. "And there are the dog-training classes I run with Christine Wilson."

"And Christine can give you information about feeding and everything," Tristan added.

"And you can do your marathon training together!" Andi pointed out. "This puppy needs lots of exercise! It'll keep her out of mischief."

"And during the day, when I'm out on my rounds, she

can keep everyone company at the post office." Mike was clearly warming to the idea. "Tony, one of the clerks, loves dogs. He'd be thrilled to keep an eye on her."

"It's perfect!" Natalie declared. "How about it, Fisher? Can Mike have her?"

The puppy stretched up and licked Mike's ear.

Fisher smiled. "Looks like she's picked out her new owner herself," he said. "And I'd hate to disappoint her."

Mike's smile stretched even wider. "Wow!" he beamed, hugging the puppy tightly. "You hear that, girl? You're coming home with me!"

"Wait right there!" said Andi, holding up her hand. "You're forgetting one very important thing!"

Mike looked up. "What? I can get her a basket and a leash on the way home, can't I?"

"Nothing like that," Andi said with a grin. "This little pup may have found her new home, but we never did find her a new name!"

ABOUT THE AUTHOR

Ben Baglio was born in New York, and grew up in a small town in southern New Jersey. He was the only boy in a family with three sisters.

Ben spent a lot of his childhood reading. English was always his favorite subject, and after graduating from high school, he went on to study English Literature at the University of Pennsylvania. During his coursework, he was able to spend a year in Edinburgh, Scotland.

After graduation, Ben Baglio worked as a children's book editor in New York City. He also wrote his first book, which was about the Olympics in ancient Greece. Five years later, he took a job at a publishing house in England.

Ben Baglio is the author of the *Dolphin Diaries* series, and is perhaps most well known for the *Animal Ark* and *Animal Ark Hauntings* series. These books were originally published in England (under the pseudonym Lucy Daniels), and have since gone on to be published in the United States and translated into 15 languages.

Aside from writing, Ben enjoys scuba diving and swimming, music and movies. He has a beagle named Bob, who is by his side whenever he writes.

Name That Dog!

~~Goldie~~
~~Fang~~
~~Ripper~~
~~Demon~~
~~Spike~~
~~Amabel~~
~~Beauty~~
?

Andi, Tristan, and Natalie tried their best but they couldn't find the perfect name for the little Labrador puppy. **Did you think of a perfect name while you were reading the book?**

Winning Name Will Be Used in Future Pet Finders Club Books!

Enter the Pet Finders Club **Name That Dog** Contest!
Write your perfect dog name on a postcard with your name, address, age, grade, and phone number. Send entries to:
**Pet Finders Club Name That Dog Contest 2005
P.O. Box 714
New York, NY 10013-0714
Entries must be received by June 10, 2005.**

1 Grand Prize-winning name will be chosen and used whenever the golden Lab appears in future Pet Finders Club stories.
PLUS, the winner will receive a set of Pet Finders Club books!
10 Runners-Up will receive a set of Pet Finders Club books!